Drifting In Numbers

Drifting In Numbers

Drifting In Numbers

Carolyn Campbell

Raven Publishing

To my grandmother,
who knew the depths of pain in this lifetime,
yet her love remained unwavering and pure.

It's almost over
It's just begun
-Bo Burnham

"People say, 'They have no idea
how bad they hurt me.'

Yes, they do, love.
They know exactly how bad they hurt you.
That's why they disappeared.
It's hard to look at someone when you know
you destroyed them.
So, don't ever think someone doesn't know.

But learn to be better than that."

-Stephanie Bennett-Henry

I told you

I would tell the world.

Drifting In Numbers

Contents

Drifting In Numbers

Violet

You made
eternity make sense.
I'm not sure
if I believe
in love
at first sight.

All I know
is that
the second my eyes
met yours,
I started counting
to infinity.

The moment
you turned your
eyes away
and walked out,
I was drifting
in numbers
that would never be counted.

You dug me a hole,
and I let you lower me down,
believing you'd join me,
that we'd share the dark,
deciding together
when to climb back to light.

I was wrong.

You stayed above,
looking down with amusement,
a trickster's grin
as I lay in the shadows,
grieving the death of who I was.

You watched my tears,
each drop a silent plea,
as you tossed shovelfuls of dirt,
burying me alive,
layer by layer,
with cruel precision.

Yet in the silence,
I remain,
entombed and unmoving,
breathing beneath the weight,
a ghost in my own skin.

We are bound by wounds,
our hearts stitched with scars,
love and hate entwined,
pulling us close, tearing us apart.

In the shadows of pain,
your touch is both balm and blade,
a tangled dance of need and fear,
where comfort bleeds into captivity.

I crave the release,
yet long for your chains,
lost in the paradox
of our haunted embrace.

She melted you down,
crafted a coward from your bones.

The embarrassment
stings, enough to spark
anger, driving me
to write it down.

I need it in ink,
a permanent reminder
to revisit
whenever I feel
pathetic again.

You married me,
chose me among the stars,
promised love and safety,
and I believed every word,
every whispered vow.

But then you sought more,
craving others' shadows,
more women to fill the void
I thought we had sealed,
leaving promises fractured
like shards of broken glass.

I
tolerated
so
much
just
so
I
got
to
keep
loving
you.

You told me to stop living in the past,
as if erasing the pain
could heal the wounds
you left inside me.

As if ignoring the scars
would mend what you broke,
silencing the echoes
of the hurt you left behind.

Stop trying to communicate,
your feelings lost on her,
irrelevant to her heart.
Stop sharing your truth,
lock it away inside.

Stay silent,
be your own best friend,
remain hidden in your mind,
whisper to yourself, not to her.

She will never understand
the you you yearn for her to see,
the part of you that longs for love,
forever unseen by her eyes.

So let her remain distant,
let her never touch the depths of you,
be cold, be distant,
it's the only way to survive.

She wants you hollow,
empty as a shell,
so become that—
be empty, be void.

Be empty for her peace,
a sacrifice for her happiness.

She looks at me
with eyes that have already judged,
decided how I feel
before a word is spoken.

Her gaze maps out
emotions I haven't yet named,
a verdict passed
without a moment's pause.

I don't want you to contact me,
to linger in my space,
I wish for your disappearance,
a silence that stretches long.

Yet, I crave your message,
the sound of your voice,
your false compassion, your false sympathy,
the comfort of your tight embrace.

I yearn for the kisses
you once sought from me,
but still, I don't want you to reach out,
to break the quiet I've wished for.

Sometimes, I close my eyes,
imagining a year from now,
when this pain will be a distant memory,
and peace, a newfound companion.

I'll look back on this moment,
longing to tell my past self
that all will be well,
that happiness is on the horizon.

In time, I'll yearn
to speak to the me who's hurting now,
to offer comfort,
and whisper softly,
"It's going to be okay.

It's going to be okay."

Words and words and words,
paragraphs spilling into pages,
an entire journal
overflowing with my heart.

I wrote for you,
poured out my feelings,
all of it
meant nothing to you.

So much ink wasted,
each drop a testament
to a silence
that swallowed my voice.

I'm not doing it anymore,
no more wasted pages,
no more long paragraphs
sent to a heart that won't believe.

This must be the end,
my final words,
etched in the silence
you've left behind.

I learned to love unconditionally
with you,
but I also learned
what it feels like
to not receive that love in return.

It broke me.

It's just a day,
one day,
perhaps tomorrow too,
but not every day
will be touched by sorrow.

Speak happiness
into existence,
and the universe
will respond.

Giving up isn't an option,
sweetheart,
keep moving forward,
and let hope guide your way.

The addiction to pen and paper
has taken hold,
a pull I cannot ignore,
grabbing the book and pen
to spill it all out.

I don't fear who might read it,
not writing for the eyes
of strangers or future selves,
nor for a child yet to come.

I am simply writing,
driven by the need
to let the words flow,
for the pure act of creation.

This morning, I woke from a dream of you,
we were curled in bed,
talking of moving to Missouri,
not as lovers, but as roommates,
keeping our distance,
to heal and reinvent ourselves.

We spoke of meeting again in a year,
reintroducing ourselves,
with time to mend,
to be who we wanted to be.
Planning the move,
a truck to be ordered in three weeks.

I held your body,
kissed your cheek,
and felt a warmth,
a sense of home,
so profound it lingered,
even as I awoke.

I missed the dream's comfort,
but found peace in its fleeting illusion,
content that it was only a dream.

You don't know it,
but we make love every night.
Every night you open the white door,
standing there, your amber eyes
piercing through me.

I wonder what fills your thoughts—
Is it me?
My legs, the paleness of my skin,
or the black lace draped across my body?
Was it any of that?

You don't know it,
but we make love every night.
Every night, you enter the bedroom,
crawl onto the bed,
hovering above me,
your gold chain swaying gently.

It was you in my thoughts,
the almond hue of your skin,
the curl of your hair around my face.
It was all of that.

Replaying in my mind,
every night,
we make love
in the deepest corners of my dreams.

I don't want you to contact me,
I want you to vanish,
to disappear from my world.

Yet, I yearn for your text,
for the sound of your voice,
your compassion, your sympathy.

I crave your tight embrace,
the kisses you once sought from me,
the comfort you offered and desired.

But still, I don't want you to reach out,
to break the silence I've wished for.

Dear Self,

You've faced heartbreak before,
perhaps not this severe,
but you've navigated sorrow—
again and again.

You know it gets better,
the sadness, the regrets, the anger,
they've all been part of your journey.
Now, it's time.

Time to lift yourself
off the cold, hard floor,
to reclaim your essence,
to be yourself again.

Love yourself in your own language,
spoil yourself without restraint,
transform chores into acts of love,
be the vibrant version of yourself.

Shit happens—
you gave her your all,
now it's time to give it to yourself.
Drive yourself to success,
because I believe in you.

Every day is a triumph,
a high, because YOU ARE HERE

I find myself reaching for pen and paper,
more often now,
even when words seem absent.
Why is this so?

What am I nurturing inside,
growing once more in the quiet?
Perhaps, I'm choosing ink over voices,
seeking no validation from others.

It feels right to pour thoughts onto pages,
to find solace in my own words,
rather than seeking ears to listen.
I'm learning to be my own best friend.

I've been dreaming of escape,
of weaving romance with my own life,
finding ways to enchant each day
with solitude's sweet embrace.

How can I craft this daily dance,
where moments sparkle with self-love,
where every day becomes a canvas
for my own delight and grace?

Perhaps it's in small, sacred acts—
a cup of coffee savored slowly,
a walk under a sky of stars,
or simply a quiet pause, alone.

Let each day be a gentle romance,
a celebration of my own company,
where I find magic in the mundane,
and cherish the art of being me.

What about Violet?

I'm indifferent now,
not angered, not saddened—
just a calm release.
I don't care about her escapades,
the laughter she shares,
or the fun she's having.

No longer burdened
by those intrusive thoughts,
I find freedom
in her absence.
The weight of our past,
our potential,
once so heavy,
has finally lifted.

I no longer yearn
for what was good,
or miss her touch,
her voice,
her smile.
The last threads of attachment
have unraveled.

I am no longer in love,
not with her, not with anyone.
My heart is my own,
breathing freely,
emerging from years of drowning.

Each day feels like a breath
of fresh air,
a testament to my healing,
as I do the work
and find peace within.

Clothed and distant,
miles away,
you ignored me
while I wept in silence.

You said you'd punch me
if I dared to speak.

I stayed silent,
and as soon as you walked out,
I called for maintenance,
to replace the lock on the door.

The soft, brown skin of your arm
wrapped around my neck,
a serpent's embrace,
tightening with a suffocating grip.

My body surrendered,
and darkness
closed in behind my eyes.

The sun blazed through the blinds
for hours,
as I gazed out,
waiting for your return.

I lay in bed, tears flowing,
all weekend for you,
while you laughed
with her,
unconcerned and free.

You'd say,
"It's the past,
move on."

But the trauma
you left behind
is a shadow I live with daily,
haunting my present
with echoes of the past.

I am caught
in a constant loop,
paranoid and weary,
unable to escape
the remnants of what was.

I fell ill,
my body weakening,
while I waited,
hollowed out
by lack of love from you.

In the quiet of my room,
I withered,
each breath a struggle,
each ache a reminder
of the care I'd hoped for.

You watched me deteriorate,
from a distance,
unmoved by my fading light.
Not a word, not a touch,
to soothe the pain
that grew with each passing hour.

I longed for you
to ease my suffering,
to bridge the gap
between hope and despair,
but you remained absent,
leaving me to grapple
with my own emptiness.

The silence grew heavy,
a stark contrast
to the care I craved,
while I remained,
untended,
lost in the echo
of what should have been.

You asked if I wanted to keep
the vows I wrote for you,
or if I should
discard them.

I wanted you
to take them to heart,
but they seemed
just a foolish declaration
from someone who loved too deeply.

So, I threw them away,
each promise a reminder
of a love
that was never truly valued.

I'm
writing
your
demise,

each word
a stroke
of finality,
each line
a chapter
of endings.

My son stood there,
his heart open,
saying, "I love you."

You looked at him,
then turned away,
and said,
"I don't want to get attached."

He's loved you
for three years,
he's been attached—
a bond you chose to ignore.

In your rage,
directed at me,
you shoved him
to the floor.

That's when I knew,
with piercing clarity,
the monster within you.

I refuse
to forgive you
for everything
you apologized for,

each word of regret
a hollow echo
against the weight
of what you've done.

I was so hungry
for your love,
I starved myself,
physically aching
for the nourishment
you failed to give.

You walked around,
letting everyone
trample over me,
while you stood aside,
watching it all unfold.

Nothing is more painful to me
than true things being denied,
truths sharp and deep,
cast aside and smothered
by disbelief and disregard.

Reality twisted,
truths buried under falsehood,
weigh heavy on my heart,
a stone pressing, suffocating
with each denial.

You say the sun isn't gold,
that stars don't burn,
that my feelings are illusions,
my memories mere mirages,
leaving me grappling
with the void of your indifference.

Every truth I speak
feels like a scream
lost in the vast silence
of your denial.

How can you see the scars
and call them shadows?
How can you ignore the truth
bare before you?

The pain of being disregarded
is an aching wound,
where my truths are trampled
by callous disregard,
and I mourn what should have been seen.

Still, I hold to my truths,
hoping someday
the walls will crumble,
the light will break through,
and the truth will be acknowledged,
amid the fog of misunderstanding.

Do I fight the depression,
or let it engulf me whole?
Do I resist the shadows,
or surrender to their pull?

Each day a battle unseen,
a struggle within the dark,
where hope flickers faintly
like a distant, wavering spark.

Do I grasp at fleeting light,
or let the shadows claim their due?
Do I cling to the edges of dawn,
or dissolve in the night's cold dew?

The unknown looms ahead,
a vast and daunting sea,
where each wave's roar
questions what's to be.

Do I take my life
and end the endless strife,
or do I fight the murky depths
and seek a glimmer of life?

In the silence of the night,
where shadows whisper low,
I wrestle with the darkness,
with no clear path to show.

Yet in this storm of doubt,
amidst the pain and fear,
I search for strength to carry on,
for hope to reappear.

For in the choice between despair
and the fight for brighter days,
I'll seek the dawn with weary heart
and navigate through the haze.

I want to explode from the inside,
crushed by the weight of knowing
she doesn't love me,
the most painful truth
of my fractured heart.

It's an ache that sears,
a realization so sharp,
that I'm the one who deserves more,
yet I keep placing her at the center,
offering all I have,
knowing it will never be enough.

I am the sunburned sky,
stretching out,
giving warmth and light,
while she drifts by,
unmoved, untouched,
leaving my heart in shadows.

Each gesture, a hollow echo,
every sacrifice, a silent scream,
fading into the void
of her indifference,
where my love is a whispered prayer
lost in the expanse of her apathy.

The explosion within me
is the sound of my own despair,
a crack splitting open
where my worth lies buried,
drowned out by the clamor
of unrequited hope.

I deserve the sun's embrace,
a heart that burns with genuine fire,
yet I remain here,
giving everything,
to someone who will never
truly see me.

She doesn't want

me.

Not the echoes of my heart
or the warmth of my embrace,
not the quiet, steadfast love
that I offer unconditionally.

She doesn't want

me.

In her eyes, I am a shadow,
a fleeting thought that drifts away,
a silent plea lost in the noise
of her indifference.

She doesn't want

me.

And so, I am left
with the empty spaces,
the silent rooms of longing,
where I realize the truth.

She doesn't want

me.

To her next lover,

Those hands of hers,
that bring you pleasure,
have left bruises on me,
marks of a love that shattered.

Beware.

They once caressed with tenderness,
now they carry scars,
etched deep where her touch
was once a promise.

Beware.

What feels warm and inviting
might carry the chill
of past wounds,
hidden beneath her allure.

Her hands are skilled,
but they've known
the art of causing pain,
as well as delight.

So tread lightly,
for what seems gentle
may hold the weight
of my broken heart.

Beware.

Do you remember that night,
when your ex came to town,
and without a notice,
you vanished at nine,
turned off your location,
blocked my number,
and left me waiting
until two the next day?

I do.

You claimed you spent
the hours in your car,
parked in some store lot,
while I wondered
if the silence
was a cruel joke.

Have you always thought
I was stupid?

Did you believe
I'd accept your story
as truth,
while my heart lay
shattered in the wake
of your disappearance?

I remember the night,
and I remember
the emptiness
of your words.

The truth, buried
under layers of deceit,
is a wound that still aches,
and I'm left grappling
with the weight
of your absence.

12:01am, I opened my eyes
in the new year,
separating my lips from yours—
confetti still falling around us.
This was the happiest I had ever felt.

Six months later, we wandered
the Garden of the Gods,
our wedding photos capturing
a fleeting joy.

Four weeks later, I lay
in my son's bed,
unable to bear the space
next to you.

Three weeks later, your hands
became a chokehold,
leaving bruises on my neck,
a physical mark of your rage.

Eight weeks later, I sit
in a coffee shop,
reading poetry alone,
lost in the echo of what was.

And I just want to go back
to 12:01am,
to try again,
to reclaim the joy
that slipped through our fingers.

You were poison,
but you tasted so good,
a bitter sweetness
I couldn't resist.

I kept drinking,
savoring the danger,
until it seeped
into my veins.

The pleasure turned
to a dark yearning,
and I found myself
wanting to kill myself,
drowning in the toxicity
of your love.

The poison became my craving,
and in your embrace,
I sought solace
even as it
wreaked havoc
within me.

I'm sorry
for all the things
I forgot I did,
the shadows of my actions
lost in the fog
of unremembered days.

Forgive me
for the moments
that slipped from my grasp,
for the hurt I caused
in my own haze,
the echoes of mistakes
I no longer see.

I am sorry
for what I can't recall,
the unintentional wounds
left behind,
and the times
I failed to mend
what I didn't remember breaking.

Let this apology
reach beyond
the forgotten spaces,
a gesture to heal
the silent scars
of my unremembered wrongs.

Being with you
was standing in a thunderstorm,
embracing the storm's fury,
loving the pain
as the lightning struck me
over
and over
and over.

Each bolt was a spark
of searing truth,
a jagged kiss
that illuminated
the storm's rage
within my heart.

The thunder roared
in the echo of your voice,
a relentless drum
beating against my chest,
as I stood,
soaked and trembling,
finding solace
in the storm's cruel embrace.

Even as the lightning
shattered the sky,
I cherished the burn,
the fierce reminder
of a love
that was both fierce
and unforgiving.

We were always going to be
two lovers
destined to destroy each other,
bound by a fate
that tangled our hearts
in a dance of ruin.

From the start,
our love was a wildfire,
burning bright and fierce,
consuming everything in its path,
leaving only ashes
of what we once were.

We clung to the flames,
embracing the heat,
even as it scorched our souls,
a fierce inevitability
that pulled us closer
while tearing us apart.

In the end,
our love was a storm
that swept through our lives,
a force of nature
that left devastation
in its wake.

We were destined
to be the architects
of our own destruction,
two hearts bound
to collapse under the weight
of a love
that could never be tamed.

You said you cried relief
the day you walked out the door
for good,
a weight lifted from your shoulders,
a burden finally released.

Then why did I have to
convince you to get off the couch
and actually go?
If relief was your beacon,
why was the exit so hard to find?

If you were so relieved,
why did every step
toward the door
feel like an ordeal,
like dragging chains
through a storm?

Was your relief
a whisper in the dark
or just a story
you told yourself
to soften the blow
of a departure
that still choked you?

You spoke of freedom
with tears in your eyes,
yet the road to leaving
was a maze of hesitation,
each moment stretching
into an eternity of doubt.

So if it was relief
that set you free,
why did the journey
to that freedom
feel like a prison,
a battle between desire
and the weight of goodbye?

Do you remember the night
you strangled me
in front of my son,
all because we wouldn't
turn the cartoons off
at 8pm?

I do.
I remember the suffocating grip
that silenced my breath,
the way your anger
screamed louder than any words
could convey.

I remember the fear in his eyes,
the confusion
etched across his small face,
as he witnessed a storm
of violence and rage
that no child should ever see.

The night etched itself
into my memory,
a dark scar that pulses
with every reminder
of what happened
when love twisted into cruelty.

You can forget if you choose,
but I hold it with me
like a cold shadow,
a permanent reminder
of the night
you let fury
take control.

Something shifted in me today,
a clarity born of chaos.
For days, she reached out—
texts, calls, even No Caller ID,
relentless in her pursuit.

I saw through the fog of her intentions,
her attempts to disrupt what I've built,
to undo the happiness I've found
with someone new.
Her sabotage was clear;
she never wanted me to be content.

She tried to lure me back,
to unravel the threads of my newfound joy,
a final act of manipulation,
her control over me
the only game she knew how to play.

But today, I severed the cord.
No more will I be her puppet,
no more her easy target.
I've seen through her guise,
and in doing so, I've freed myself.

The end is here,
a fresh start in the wake of her deceit.
For I am finally free—
a person who chooses their own path,
unshackled from the past
that she tried so hard to bind.

Today was hard,
a day drenched in shadows,
where "bad" was the only label
that fit my mood.

It was the first time in ages
I allowed myself to feel
the weight of the day,
to embrace the depth
of my own despair.

But then, a spark ignited,
a reminder of who I am—
the strength I wield,
the magic I conjure,
the resilience that lives
in every corner of my being.

I grew angry with myself,
not for feeling, but for forgetting,
and let go of the heaviness
that had settled too long.
I hit the gym,
channeling my pain into motion,
my breath a testament to renewal.

Tomorrow, I reclaim myself.
With each sunrise, I will be back—
stronger, brighter,
a force of my own making,
ready to face the world again
with the power of my own truth.

I've been questioning for months
if depression has wrapped its arms around me.
Am I?
It feels different, a new kind of shadow.

I'm not weeping in the night,
nor am I haunted by the thought of ending things.
I don't feel the tears,
yet I wonder if the emptiness within is its own kind of
sorrow.

I'm numb.
Joy has slipped through my fingers,
a ghost of what once was.
Sleep eludes me,
only three hours of rest each night,
a whisper of what I need.

I struggle to tend to my own space,
a battleground of clutter and dust,
where even my hobbies become burdens,
shadows of the pleasure they once brought.

I don't wish for death,
merely a return to a life
where happiness isn't a distant dream
but a tangible reality.
I want to feel again,
to reclaim the spark that's faded,
to find solace and joy
beyond this numbness.

I want to be happy again.
I want to find the warmth
in the corners of my soul
and to live fully, once more.

On the first, I lit two candles,
one bearing your name,
one with mine,
tied together by a ribbon of intent.

I watched the flames intertwine,
their dance a silent promise
to release and renew.

The next morning, I awoke
to a shift within.
I no longer missed you,
no longer felt the ache
that once constricted my chest,
searching for the reasons,
the understanding that eluded me.

I ceased my obsession
with the fragments of you,
the questions and the pain.

Suddenly, in the quiet dawn,
my head and heart found stillness,
a peace unfound before,
a calm where there was once tumult.

The candles had burned away
more than wax and wick;
they had dispelled the shadows
that haunted my soul,
leaving me with the silence
I needed to heal.

I feel this layer of skin I'm shedding,
a veil of toxic traits,
once clung to me like a second skin,
woven from the threads of her deceit.

Each day, I peel away the remnants,
a revelation of who I am beneath,
stripped of the shadows she cast,
the fears and doubts she seeded.

The old skin, now discarded,
holds the echoes of her manipulations,
her anger and her indifference,
an imprint on my very soul.

As I shed it, I feel lighter,
each layer falling away
reveals the truth of my own strength,
the resilience I forgot I had.

With each breath, I reclaim myself,
rebuilding from the pieces
of the self she tried to obscure,
finding the clarity in the space she left.

I am reborn from the remnants,
emerging into a truth
untouched by her darkness,
a testament to the healing
that comes from finally letting go.

The last time you walked out
the front door,
I exhaled a breath
I had been holding
for three years.

It was as if I had been
underwater,
breathing in the weight
of your departure,
and finally, I surfaced.

That breath, long trapped
in the depths of my chest,
unfurled into freedom,
filling the spaces
you had once occupied.

I felt the air rush
through my lungs,
a cleansing wind,
whispering of release
and the promise of renewal.

In that moment,
I was no longer tethered
to your shadow,
no longer imprisoned
by the past's suffocating grip.

I embraced the light
that flooded in,
finding solace
in the empty space
where you used to be.

Everyone kept asking me
if I was okay.

I kept telling them all,
"It feels like I finally
came up for air."

As if I had been submerged
in the depths of a stormy sea,
held beneath the waves
of heartache and doubt,
struggling for a breath
that never seemed to come.

Each question, a reminder
of the weight I carried,
each answer, a gasp of relief,
a declaration of newfound freedom.

I told them, "It feels like I finally
came up for air,"
for in those words,
was the truth of my liberation—
the freedom from the abyss
where I had been lost.

No longer bound
by the pressure of the depths,
I could breathe deeply,
feeling the sun on my face,
embracing the calm of the surface,
and finding peace
in the vast expanse of the sky.

I had been drowning for years,
lost beneath the weight
of shared debts and broken promises.

When the last bill,
our final tether,
was transferred to my name,
I felt a shift—

a crack in the relentless waves,
a chance to break through.

I pushed upwards,
fighting against the currents
that had held me down,
and when I broke through the surface,

I took a gulp of air,
the first breath of freedom
in what felt like an eternity.

In that moment,
the water receded,
and I was alive,
breathing deeply,
feeling the sky
spread out before me,
no longer shackled
by the weight of the past.

In bed at 10pm,
I turn the pages of poetry,
lost in verses
while you drift through my thoughts.

What are you doing tonight?
Are you asleep?
Working out?
At your mom's place?
Or, as whispers tell me,
drinking again,
a habit that clings to you
like an old, stubborn shadow?

Some things never change,
even as my world shifts
and I find solace
in the quiet of my room,
surrounded by words
that offer comfort
more enduring than your presence.

Our mutual friends
still speak of you,
a parade of updates
I hear in passing.
I smile,
a knowing smirk,
as they recount your latest drama,
the same old storylines
that once held me captive.

I laugh,
a genuine burst of mirth,
for the truth is,
I couldn't care less
about your existence now.
Your name,
once a constant in my thoughts,
is just a distant echo,
a whisper drowned out
by the sound of my own liberation.

One of these days,
I'll wake up and find
your name no longer
a ghost in my notebook,
a shadow in my ink.
The pages will turn,
free of the weight
of our past,
unburdened by the lines
that once dripped with sorrow.

I'll write new tales,
fresh ink on clean sheets,
where your memory
no longer tugs
at the edges of my words,
no longer seeps
into the marrow of my verses.

One of these days,
the poems will flow
without the echo
of your voice,
without the shadow
of your absence,
and I'll finally discover
the silence that follows
when your story is truly over.

I don't really have much left
to say to you,
or even about you.

You've become
a footnote,
a flicker in the distance
of my past,
irrelevant
as the whispers of yesterday's wind.

Your name no longer
dances on my lips,
nor do your memories
linger like ghosts.

I've sifted through
the wreckage of what was,
and found
that what remains
is an emptiness
that doesn't ache.

You've become
a silent void,
a blank page
in the book
of my life,
and I've moved on
to write
new chapters
where you have no place.

It was your name
in the main subject line
of my thoughts,
every morning,
all day,
until I closed my eyes
at night, and even then,
I fell asleep
concerned with my relationship
with you.

Your presence
was a constant headline,
a breaking news
that never faded,
an obsession
etched into every waking moment
and every sleepless hour.

I would weave dreams
around your name,
an endless narrative
that left me tangled
in the web of us,
until finally,
the pages of my mind
could no longer bear
the weight of your story.

Now,
I sift through the echoes
of what was,
finding peace
in the quiet
of a new dawn
where your name
no longer
shouts for attention.

My physical body was traveling
about the space
in which it needed to
survive—but my soul,
my thoughts,
my inner existence
lay lifeless somewhere
in the dark,
haunted by what you
put me through.

Each step forward
was a motion,
a shadow of life
moving through the motions
while my spirit remained
bound by the echoes
of your touch,
your words,
the lingering specters
of a love turned nightmare.

PTSD, a silent companion,
clung to me in every shadow,
casting doubt and fear
in the corners of my mind,
a constant reminder
of battles fought within,
where peace seemed
a distant memory.

Yet still, I wander,
searching for the light
in the dim corridors
of my own existence,
yearning for the day
when the echoes fade,
when the darkness
gives way to dawn,
and my soul reclaims
the life
it was meant to lead.

Dear Violet,

If I were to write you a letter,
what would I say?
I've said everything
and more than I should have
while we were together.
What difference would words make now?

Nothing.
Words mean nothing to you,
no weight to someone
who uses them to manipulate
and benefit themselves.

The difference between us—
I am full of love and light.
You are an empty shell
of a human,
devoid of warmth,
a hollow echo
of what could have been.

I've learned to embrace
the radiance within me,
while you remain lost,
trapped in the shadows
of your own making.

I'm learning to silence
the voices within,
the echoes of doubt
that threaten to consume.

No longer allowing thoughts
to claw at my spirit,
tear at my flesh,
a battle between the mind
and the vessel it inhabits.

I'm refusing to let my mind
destroy the body it dwells in,
fighting back with resilience,
embracing the strength
of my own existence.

I am not a prisoner
of my own thoughts.
I am the guardian
of my body's sanctuary,
protecting it fiercely
from the storms within.

You tripped over my insecurities
despite how I had deliberately
placed them well out of your way.

Carefully tucked into corners,
hidden from sight,
I hoped you'd navigate
with care,
avoid the tangled roots
of my fears and doubts.

But you stumbled,
unconcerned with the wreckage,
disregarding the caution
I took to keep you safe
from the depths
of my vulnerabilities.

I watched as you trampled
through the spaces
I kept sacred,
realizing too late
that my efforts
to protect us both
were in vain.

It seemed no matter how hard I tried
to avoid conflict or disagreements,
to be pleasant and agreeable,
I still wasn't being the right
human for you.

Every step, a careful dance
around your temper's edge,
tiptoeing on eggshells,
yet I faltered in your eyes,
never quite enough.

I twisted myself into shapes
that felt unnatural,
silenced my voice to be
what you desired,
but still fell short.

The mirror reflected someone
I hardly recognized,
bent and contorted,
a version of me
lost in your expectations.

Yet, I learned that rightness
isn't found in surrendering
myself for your comfort,
but in the courage to be
the human I truly am.

Your presence put me on edge,
with your dramatics
and little tantrums
when you didn't get your way.

Every sigh, every glare,
a spark in a tinderbox,
igniting tension in the air
as I braced for the storm
of your displeasure.

Your voice, sharp as glass,
cut through moments of peace,
turning calm into chaos,
until walking on eggshells
felt like home.

I tiptoed through conversations,
gauging each word, each pause,
fearing the eruption
that simmered beneath
your surface.

In your shadow,
I lost my balance,
struggling to stand firm
against the gusts
of your whims.

Yet, in the end,
it was your own tempest
that unraveled the ties,
and set me free
from the edge.

You made me doubt
what I knew to be true,
twisting reality
into knots of confusion,
where clarity once lived.

Your words spun webs
of deceit and uncertainty,
a tangled dance of half-truths
and contradictions
that left me questioning
my own mind.

There is a word
for people like you,
those who blur the lines
between light and shadow,
casting doubt as a tool
to bend the world
to their will.

Manipulator,
master of the game,
you played my trust
like a puppet on strings,
pulling me into
your labyrinth of lies.

But now I see the threads,
the intricate design
of your deception,
and I step away
from the maze
you crafted.

Truth finds its way
through the cracks,
and I reclaim
the certainty
you tried to steal,
knowing the word
that defines
what you are.

You lied about your ex
being in my apartment
while I was in Europe,
your deceit woven
into the fabric
of our shared life.

Yet you twisted the truth,
turning tables
with practiced ease,
manipulating my heart
into groveling and begging
for forgiveness.

You spun tales of innocence
as I accused you,
your words a tangled web
that ensnared my mind,
casting shadows of doubt
where clarity should have been.

I became the villain
in your crafted narrative,
a marionette dancing
to your tune of contrition,
while the truth hid
beneath layers of falsehood.

But now I see the pattern,
the skillful art
of your manipulation,
and I stand firm
in the light of truth,
no longer a pawn
in your game of deceit.

I called you beautiful,
funny,
kind,
supportive,
the love of my life,
words that tumbled
from my lips
in hopeful sincerity.

Yet beneath each compliment,
a quiet discord thrummed,
an undercurrent of unease
that whispered of truths
I couldn't quite grasp,
even as I tried
to embrace the illusion.

Despite how bad I felt
in your company every day,
I clung to the image
of who I wanted you to be,
the reflection of a love
I desperately sought
in the shifting shadows.

But the heart knows
what the mind denies,
and the weight of falsehood
bore down,
pressing against the facade
until the cracks
became too wide to ignore.

I see now the difference
between what I wished for
and the reality we lived,
and I release the words,
the labels,
the illusions,
to find the truth
that lay beneath.

The perfect version of you
was just an illusion
I conjured in my mind,
a delicate fantasy
I fell in love with,
crafted from dreams
and desires
that danced
in the corners of my heart.

I painted you
in hues of idealism,
a masterpiece
of imagined virtues,
a figure of flawless grace
that I desperately wanted
to believe was real.

But behind the veil
of my own creation,
the truth lay hidden,
a shadow of imperfections
that didn't fit
the portrait I adored.

In loving the image,
I neglected the essence,
the flawed reality
that didn't match
the perfection
I had spun from my hopes.

Now I see clearly
that the perfect version
was a mirage,
a reflection of my own longing
that dissipated
with the dawn of truth,
leaving me to face
the genuine you,
and the heartache
of my own illusions.

I felt trapped and obligated
to stay with you,
a prisoner of my own making,
bound by the chains
of my love for you.

Your presence was a cage,
its bars fashioned from affection
and yearning,
a paradox of freedom
held captive by desire.

In loving you,
I bound myself
to a fate
that was as confining
as it was consuming,
each moment a reminder
of the weight
of my own commitment.

Though I longed for escape,
my heart kept me tethered,
a compass spinning
in circles of devotion,
unable to find the direction
of my own liberation.

The love I held
was a double-edged sword,
both shelter and snare,
a paradox of passion
that left me ensnared
in the labyrinth
of my own making,
struggling to reconcile
the freedom I sought
with the chains
I chose to wear.

Every time you claimed you loved me,
I hid more of myself away,
a fragile part of me
slowly dying inside.

I buried my pain
beneath layers of pretense,
masking the parts
that withered in the shadows,
fearing that if you glimpsed
the darkness within,
your love would fade
like the morning mist.

In your embrace,
I felt the need to conceal
the fractures and scars,
to present a version
of myself unblemished,
a façade of wholeness
while my spirit
crumbled silently.

I feared that if you saw
the truth behind the mask,
the broken pieces
that made up my soul,
you would turn away,
leaving me to face
the remnants of what was lost,
alone in the silence
of my own despair.

So I kept my heart hidden,
fading more with each lie,
a ghost of the person
I once was,
trapped between the need
to be loved
and the fear
of losing it all.

You liked it when I felt small
and worthless,
a shadow of myself,
barely clinging to the edge,
a bit suicidal.

In my fragility,
you found your strength,
a twisted sense of victory
in my brokenness.

It was easier for you to be the hero
when I was on my knees,
a broken puzzle piece
you could claim to mend
with your empty promises,
a facade of savior.

You thrived in my despair,
feeding off my weakness,
turning my pain into your triumph,
dressing your ego
in the guise of compassion.

You reveled in the power
of my silent suffering,
a dark play where you
were the shining knight,
while I remained
a silent victim
in the shadows of your glory.

You needed me to falter,
to lose myself completely,
so you could be the hero
who saved the day,
while I became nothing more
than a footnote in your story.

Today, I keep having flashbacks
of when you kicked me
in the stomach so hard
that I crumpled to the ground,
my body folding in on itself
like a broken doll.

You left me there,
alone on the floor,
clutching my pain,
a silent witness to your cruelty,
while you simply walked out,
leaving destruction in your wake.

Later, you claimed
you blacked out,
that it wasn't you
who had delivered that blow,
that the memory
was a mere shadow
you couldn't recall.

I find myself caught
between the jagged edges
of my PTSD
and the cold calculation
of your narcissism.

Which is more intriguing?
The shattering echoes
of my own mind
or the chilling emptiness
of your self-serving denial?

In the end,
I am left to grapple
with the scars you've left
and the question
of which pain
is the more profound—
the wounds on my soul
or the darkness of your heart.

I bet you told everyone
I am the crazy one,
the unstable heart
in a sea of calm,
the tempest
while you played the role
of serene and steady.

I bet you painted me
as the chaos
in your carefully curated world,
the one who lost control,
the one who couldn't
keep it together.

You spun tales
of my erratic mind
and skewed reality,
while you stood
in the center,
unchanged and blameless,
a portrait of virtue
in your own narrative.

I wonder
how many believed
the stories you wove,
how many saw
the illusion
and never glimpsed
the truth behind the curtain.

But deep down,
I know the real story—
the one you tried to rewrite,
the truth you twisted
to fit your needs,
the truth that still
lives within me,
despite the lies
you spread.

Where is the girl I was before you?
I remember her like an old friend,
a face from a photograph
that time has faded,
yet I cannot reach through the haze
to ask her to return.

She was a spark of light
before your shadow loomed,
a soul unburdened,
brimming with dreams
and laughter that danced
in the corners of her eyes.

Now, I stand in her absence,
a stranger to the mirror,
searching for echoes
of her voice in the silence,
wondering how to bridge the gap
between who I was
and who I've become.

How do I contact her
when the number has changed,
when the lines have blurred,
and the connection
seems lost in the static
of my present despair?

I yearn to reach out
to that version of myself
who knew how to live
without fear,
who moved through the world
with grace and certainty.

But all I have are fragments,
a memory of her warmth
that now feels distant,
like a faded star
that once lit up my nights.

So, I stand here,
wondering how to coax her back,
how to invite her
to step once more
into the life
that's been altered
by your presence and departure.

For now, I hope
that somewhere in the echoes,
the girl I was still lingers,
waiting for the chance
to reclaim her place
and remind me
of who I truly am.

I still cry because the PTSD
destroyed my favorite version of myself,
the one who danced freely in the light,
before shadows fell and stole her grace.

She was vibrant,
a soul unburdened by the past,
a beacon of joy
that once filled the room
with laughter and hope.

Now, in her place,
a ghost of what once was
wanders through the ruins,
haunted by echoes
of pain and fear.

The girl who used to dream
is lost in the wreckage,
her brightness dimmed
by the weight of trauma,
her spirit fractured,
scattered like shards of glass.

I mourn her with every tear,
grieve the loss of a self
that was whole and untainted,
now shattered by the scars
left behind by what you did.

Yet, even as I weep,
I hold a flicker of hope,
a fragile ember
that she might yet be found,
reborn from the ashes,
and given back the life

she once knew.

Until then, I carry her memory,
a reminder of the person
I still long to be,
as I navigate through the remnants
of a shattered self,
seeking solace
in the fragments of who I was.

I was light,
carefree and full of passion
for my life,

a soul dancing
in the radiance of her own joy,
unburdened by shadows
and untroubled by doubt.

But then I met you,
the thief of identity,
who stole the brightness
from my days
and cast a veil of darkness
over my once vibrant spirit.

You came with your charm,
a veneer of affection,
and slowly, imperceptibly,
you unraveled the fabric
of who I was,
thread by thread,
until only echoes
of my former self remained.

No longer was I the light,
the carefree dreamer,
but a shadow
of my own creation,
consumed by the weight
of your presence,
struggling to reclaim
the passion
that once fueled my heart.

In your wake,

I became a ghost
of the person I was,
haunted by the memory
of a life once lived
in full color,
now faded to grayscale
by your insidious touch.

Yet, as I stand in the remnants
of what you left behind,
I cling to the hope
that I might find
the light within again,
reclaim the passion
that was stolen,
and emerge from the shadows
as the person
I was always meant to be.

When I picture myself happy,
it's a vision of the distant future,
a shimmering mirage on the horizon,
a guiding star through the dark.

I see myself there,
smiling in sunlight,
unburdened by past sorrows,
basking in joy that feels like a dream.

The weight of struggles lifted,
standing tall in contentment,
the future I long for
no longer just hope but promise.

For now, I cling to this vision,
a beacon in the fog,
guiding me toward the happiness
that awaits in the embrace of tomorrow.

The last time we spoke in person,
I approached you with kindness,
treating you with the respect
that you had not always shown me.

I offered my words gently,
my gestures calm,
hoping to bridge the chasm
that had widened between us.

Yet you met my efforts
with a storm of anger,
your voice rising like thunder,
crashing over me with sharp words.

You yelled at me,
not as if I were a fellow human,
but as if I were a disobedient dog,
a creature to be commanded and scolded.

In that moment,
I felt the sting of your disregard,
the weight of your disdain,
as if my kindness was a mere provocation
for your wrath.

I owe you nothing,
not for the days you abandoned me
or the nights you left me in shadows.

Your promises have turned to dust,
your betrayals and broken trust
crushed like fragile glass.

You speak with daggers,
your anger a weapon,
your disregard for my efforts clear.

Each glance reveals your own turmoil,
your pain a chain binding me
in the darkness of your grief.

Your true character is evident
in the coldness you show,
the lack of empathy you possess.

I owe you nothing for the scars
or the wounds of your cruel disregard.
I walk away, unburdened,
leaving behind the shadows
of your discontent,
finding freedom in my own light.

I tried for peace the last time I saw you,
hoping for a conversation free of conflict.
But your issues, your reasons,
are not my burden to bear,
nor are they excuses for your behavior.

An apology from you now
feels hollow,
a mere formality,
for it's clear that the monster inside
is who you've become.

You haven't changed.
You've made no effort to heal
the demons that haunt your heart.
The ugliness remains,
unwilling to let go.

Your lack of growth
is a reflection of the person you are,
unchanged and unrepentant,
leaving me with no choice
but to walk away.

I see myself dancing and laughing,
slow motion and bathed in a yellow filter,
a memory crafted from longing,
never lived, but conjured in my mind.

The joy is vivid,
a picture-perfect illusion,
where moments sparkle
in the warmth of a dream,
unreachable yet vivid,
as if I had once truly danced
beneath a golden sky.

This imagined happiness
is a gentle trick of the heart,
a fantasy woven from what might have been,
a tender escape from reality,
where I am free to revel
in the light of a memory
that never was.

You gave up when I was still
buying you flowers,
delivering them with a smile
that sought to brighten your days.

I greeted you with a hug
each time you came home,
offering warmth in the doorway,
a gesture of love unreciprocated.

At restaurants, I opened your straws,
a small act of care
that went unnoticed,
like a whisper lost in the wind.

I asked for dates,
hoping to rekindle the spark,
seeking moments of joy
to share with you.

But as I poured my heart
into these simple acts,
you were already gone,
your presence faded
long before I had finished giving.

In my attempts to hold on,
I remained unaware
that the love I offered
was met with silence,
and that my gestures
were only shadows
of what could have been.

I feel ugly when the darkness creeps
back in and takes over my mind.
There must be something wrong,
for it hasn't been this alright
for a very long time.

Something isn't right,
something is off.
The light that once filled me
seems distant, like a dream
fading in the early dawn.

The obscurity
carries a weight
that settles deep within,
a haunting refrain
of what I fear I've lost.

I search for the flicker
of hope within,
but it feels obscured,
hidden beneath layers
of uncertainty and confusion.

In this creeping dark,
I question the balance
of my own heart and mind,
wondering if the peace
I once felt was merely a lie,
a fleeting illusion
in the depth of the night.

Her in a cotton shirt,
a picture of simplicity,
grace untouched
by any gesture.

Her hair falls
like constellations drifting
across the night sky,
a cascade of elegance
that dances like stars
in the way famous people
move with effortless allure.

Now, I miss
the quiet elegance
of those moments,
each detail a memory
etched in the contours
of longing,
where her presence lingers
in the stillness,
a silent echo
of a beauty
that once graced my world.

Cold, bored, and hungry
from the emptiness of boredom,
I find myself trapped
in the confines of a wasted day.

I don't want to step outside,
nor do I wish to drown
in the digital noise
of my phone's screen.

The irritation settles in,
a heavy weight of frustration
that this entire Saturday
slipped away,
squandered by someone else's choice
to let time slip through our fingers,
leaving me with nothing
but a sense of squandered moments
and a gnawing annoyance
that today, of all days,
could have been something more.

I'm lost in a fog,
my mind shrouded in a haze
where clarity is elusive,
and the weight of thought
is too heavy to bear.

All I can grasp
is the sheer exhaustion
of not wanting to think anymore,
a desire to escape
the relentless churn
of endless contemplation.

In this murky blur,
I yearn for stillness,
for a respite from the relentless
whirl of my mind,
to find solace in silence
and peace in the absence
of thought's persistent hum.

I long to rise into the sky,
to find you there in quiet seclusion.
I want to watch the wind
gently stir your hair,
dancing softly around your face.

I want to reach out,
and feel your hand
reach back to mine,
as our souls converge
in the serene expanse above the clouds.

In that tranquil space,
where the world below fades away,
I yearn for us to be tender,
to rediscover the softness
we once shared,
gentle and unburdened,
floating together in the quiet of the heavens.

The cool Fall wind brushes my cheeks,
stirring memories of afternoons
wrapped in white bedsheets with you,
rain's gentle rhythm lulling us
in and out of dreams,
our bodies tangled in warm embrace.

Each drop was a soft caress,
a lullaby that guided us
through shared solace,
a cocoon of peace
from the world outside.

Now, as the wind sweeps by,
I drift back to those serene days,
cherishing the fleeting harmony
we found in each other's arms,
beneath the gentle murmur
of the rain and rustling leaves.

If there is one thing I have learned,
it is that I cannot balance my own emotions
and someone else's. In the dance of feelings,
I find my steps faltering, trying to hold
the weight of another's storm
while my own winds rage within.

The scales of my heart tip unevenly,
teetering between your turmoil
and my fragile peace. I stretch
to accommodate the space
where your pain intersects with my solace,
but the equilibrium eludes me, slipping through.

In the end, I understand that my journey
is to navigate my own tides,
to steady my course without losing
myself to the ebb and flow
of another's heart. Balance comes
not from merging worlds but from anchoring
in the certainty of my own.

I ache when I miss you,
a hollow pang that reverberates
through my chest, an echo
of moments that once felt whole.
Yet with each pang, a bitter aftertaste
of shame rises within,
reminding me of the chains
we forged in our tangled past.

Disgust settles in the pit of my stomach
when I recall our trauma bond,
the twisted threads that bound us
in pain and need. I loathe the way
I once clung to the familiarity
of our shared darkness,
how I mistook it for closeness
when it was merely a prison.

In the quiet moments of reflection,
I grapple with the remnants of what was,
feeling the ache of absence
mingled with the sting of self-reproach.
I yearn for the clarity to disentangle
my heart from the scars
that once bound us together
and find solace in the space
where healing begins.

My playlist spans 442 songs,
a sprawling map of memories,
each track a reminder of us—
a symphony of what we once were.

Every note carries a fragment
of our shared past,
a soundtrack to the moments
we lived and breathed together.

In the melodies and lyrics,
I find echoes of our laughter,
the highs and lows
that defined our time.

Violet,

Had the path been different,
I would have chosen to stay.
In another life,
you might have been the one
I envisioned spending forever with,
had you found the help you needed.

Now I see you struggled
with demons I couldn't fight for you.
Still, I will pray you overcome them
and find the peace you seek within your soul.

I see the bitterness in your posts,
a reflection of the hurt you carry.
I hope one day you move beyond that pain,
and find a way to heal and grow.

I'm ready now to love anew,
to embrace a future untainted
by the echoes of our past.
As if you, and all my former loves,
never existed.

I pray you take care.

Violet,

I've penned so many words for you,
letters from the days we first met,
a journal filled in Europe,
notes on my phone, never sent.
But above all, I wrote my vows to you,
the truest words I've ever crafted.
I wonder if you still have them,
or if they're lost to time.

Today, I find myself missing you
more than I have since the day you left.
You don't need to respond;
you don't have to reach out.
Yet, I am paralyzed by my love for you,
unable to file for divorce,
even knowing we are toxic for one another.
My soul can't let go.

Every time my phone rings,
I hope it's you.
I wait for your name on the screen,
longing for you to knock on my door.
I hate that I feel this way,
and I hope this longing fades.
You've been so hard to love,
not giving back what I needed.
I hope you find healing,
and I'm working on letting go,
because I'm exhausted from the pain,
from never feeling enough.

—Your Wife

Because of her,
I shifted from
victim
to
villain.

No longer bound
by the chains of the past,
I refuse
to ever be
the victim
again.

It always makes me smile
when I open our chat
and find you already there,
like arriving late to a date
to see you waiting,
a warm presence at the table,
ready to share our moment.

I want to know you
like a TV show
that never airs its final episode,
where every season
brings new layers,
endless storylines,
and each moment
is a chance to discover
more of the plot
and the depths of your heart.

I had planned it for weeks,
to see her, to find escape.
I needed the break,
to gaze upon her face,
to be enveloped in her presence.

At first, it felt like friendship,
tinged with apprehension,
her quiet, cute, accommodating ways
making me feel safe,
safe in a manner I never felt
with Violet.

With Charlotte,
I could share secrets
I'd kept buried deep,
safe in her ease and kindness,
her thoughtful quirks.

She has seen all the classic films,
loves music with a passionate heart,
reads poetry with a gentle touch,
snuggles with her cat,
texts good morning with warmth,
and her voice is a melody
I crave daily.

In her, I find my peace.

I'm somewhere in between,
straddling the line
between loving the discovery
of my own self,
and the joy of unraveling
the layers of you.

Each step towards self-love
is a dance with my own reflection,
a journey of understanding
the contours of my being,
while simultaneously
being drawn to the intricacies
of your soul.

In this space between,
I find a delicate balance,
a harmony of personal growth
and shared discovery,
where loving myself
meets the wonder
of loving you.

It is a place where I am
both the explorer and the guide,
navigating the landscape
of my own heart
while charting the course
through the depths of yours.

She had a beautiful bouquet
delivered to my front door today,
each blossom a silent testament
to the moments we've yet to share.

The note, simple yet profound,
read, "To getting to know you,"
a promise wrapped in petals,
a gesture of anticipation
and the beginning of something new.

The flowers spoke in colors
and fragrant whispers,
a fragrant harbinger
of the connection we are
on the cusp of discovering,
where each bloom
mirrors the unfolding
of our own story.

She lingers in the back of my mind,
a gentle presence that whispers softly,
reminding me of my own path to happiness,
that I am free to seek joy
without dedicating all my energy
to making her smile.

Her place in my thoughts is like a steady flame,
warming me in moments of solitude,
a quiet reassurance
that I can embrace life fully,
without the weight of expectation
to keep her content.

I cherish the balance she brings,
a reassuring constant
while I immerse myself in self-discovery,
knowing she waits patiently
for when I am ready
to direct my focus and energy
toward her and the promise
of what we might build together.

For now, she is my anchor
in the space between my growth and our potential,
a beacon that guides me
as I work on becoming whole,
until the time comes
when we can share our lives
with the commitment
we both deserve.

Your voice stirs a longing
deep within me,
a feeling of missing
a place I can't quite name.

It tugs at my heartstrings,
evoking memories of a home
I've never truly known,
a sanctuary I yearn for
but cannot define.

In your words,
I sense echoes of a comfort
that feels both familiar
and elusive,
a home that exists
just beyond the reach of memory.

Your voice holds a promise
of a place where I belong,
a home that slips
through the cracks of my consciousness,
reminding me of what
I've always sought
but never quite found.

I need to check in with myself
more often,
to pause and listen
to the voice of my soul
and the quiet calls of my heart.

In the rush of days and duties,
I lose sight of the small,
precious moments
that anchor me to who I am.
I need to slow down,
to reflect and reconnect
with the core of my being,
to nurture the silence
that speaks louder than the noise.

I must seek out the stillness
that holds my truth,
to remember that within
the chaos and the clutter,
there is a space
where my spirit rests,
waiting for me to return
and simply be.

I'm not familiar with your lips,
but I could become accustomed
to their delicate touch against mine,
learning the rhythm
of their gentle caress.
In the dance of our closeness,
each kiss would unfold like a new chapter,
a tender exploration
of the uncharted contours
of our shared affection.

And she reaches
for my hand
in all the moments
I wished you had.
Her touch fills the spaces
left vacant by your absence,
each clasp a gentle reminder
of the warmth I longed for,
a reflection of what could have been,
now softly realized
in her embrace.

Exposed,
on top of me,
she demanded
that I tell her
what was wrong.

Clothed,
miles apart,
you ignored
my silent pleas,
knowing I was crying.

I didn't ask the universe to replace you,
I begged it for you to love me,
to fill the void left by your absence,
to heal the wound that your departure carved.

I pleaded for a sign, a spark,
anything to show that you cared,
that you could feel the depth of my longing
and respond with the tenderness I craved.

Instead, the universe offered me someone new,
a soul whose love isn't a mere substitute,
but a genuine embrace of the affection I sought,
a balm for the heartache that once was yours.

In their presence, I find a reflection of the love
I wished for, a warmth that wraps around me
with the sincerity and care you failed to give.
Their touch is not a replacement, but a gift,
a testament to the fact that while you could not love
me,
someone else could.

She's everything I want in this life,
a radiant presence that fills my days
with joy and contentment.

Yet, despite this cherished reality,
I'll still search for you
in the murmurs of the next life,
wondering if destiny holds
a place for us beyond this existence.

In every moment of this life's embrace,
her love is my anchor,
but the remnants of our unfinished story
linger in the spaces between heartbeats,
waiting for another chance
in the realms yet unseen.

Silently, tears fell from my eyes,
each drop a muted confession
of my hidden anguish.
In the stillness of the dark,
where words failed and light faltered,
her perceptive heart
sensed the unspoken truth.

Even without sight,
her understanding reached out
across the silence,
an empathetic warmth
that cut through the shadows.
She knew I was not okay,
a quiet acknowledgment
that held more comfort
than a thousand reassurances.

In the midst of my solitude,
her presence was a gentle anchor,
a reminder that even in the darkest hours,
someone could still see beyond
the veil of my pain,
offering solace and a connection
that transcended the quiet of the night.

Laying bare
in my bedsheets,
I heard her whimper,
a prelude to the tears
that were yet to come.
In that moment,
nothing felt heavier
than the weight of her sorrow,
as if her pain was a shadow
that darkened the space between us.

Her quiet sobs
pierced through the stillness,
a poignant reminder
of the heartache we shared.
I ached with the knowledge
that my presence could not
ease her grief,
that I could only witness
the depth of her sadness
without the power to mend.

In the silence that followed,
my own sorrow mingled
with the echoes of her cries,
and the emptiness of the night
seemed to amplify
the unspoken words
and unresolved feelings
that lingered in the room.

I never want to hear her cry,
not because I lack sensitivity
to her feelings,
but because the thought
of her sadness is unbearable.
It's not the sound of her tears
that pains me,
but the knowledge
that she is so deeply hurt
that she must weep.

Her cries are not merely
sounds of distress,
but echoes of a pain
I wish I could shield her from.
Each tear she sheds
is a reminder
of the heartache I cannot
easily mend,
of the moments when
her sorrow becomes
a reflection of my own
unfulfilled desire to protect.

In the quiet spaces between
her cries and my helplessness,
I yearn for a world
where she is free from such sorrow,
where her happiness
is never marred by the need
for tears to cleanse her grief.

She laid down beside me,
rested her hand on my cheek,
her touch a gentle caress
that spoke volumes.

She smiled a heavenly smile,
a soft glow of warmth and light,
and in that moment,
I knew she loved me,
without a word spoken.

In her eyes, I saw a promise,
a quiet assurance of belonging,
a connection so profound
that it needed no explanation,
just the certainty of her love.

I don't know what love looked like with her ex's,
what words were spoken or promises made,
but the way she lights up,
as if she's found paradise when we're together,
tells me it was never as authentic as ours.

Her laughter rings like a new melody,
her eyes hold a spark that seems brand new,
and I see in her every touch and glance
a story that never felt quite right before.

Perhaps the past was a faded dream,
a series of almosts and maybes,
but now, with every shared moment,
she embraces the genuine reality we've built.

When we first began talking,
she texted me from home,
sipping peanut butter whiskey,
while I was out with strangers,
trying to drown the loneliness.

Now, she sits in my bed,
wearing nothing but underwear and a t-shirt,
peanut butter whiskey in hand,
while I search for the perfect movie,
content in our quiet togetherness.

From distant texts to shared silences,
we've traded the noise of empty nights
for the comfort of closeness,
finding solace in each other's presence,
redefining what it means to be home.

If her exes are reading this,
know she's now being properly loved.
Her laughter rings through rooms,
filling spaces once silent.

She wears happiness like a second skin,
radiant and unrestrained,
embracing the freedom
of being wholly seen and cherished.

In our moments together,
there's no shadow of doubt,
only the light of genuine connection
and the warmth of mutual care.

Rest assured,
her heart is safe and flourishing,
held with the tenderness
she's always deserved.

I'm not 'trying' to be petty,
it comes naturally,
like an instinct woven
into my thoughts,
a reflex in the presence
of irritation or slight.

A sharp tongue dances
without hesitation,
casting shade with ease,
a gentle smirk betraying
my subtle mischief.

I navigate the world
with a wry humor,
turning small slights
into playful banter,
not with malice,
but with a wink
and a knowing nod,
embracing the art
of being unbothered.

I wondered why I was addressing her
directly with 'you,'
while you remained
in the shadows as 'her.'
I'm sorry for the oversight.

She doesn't deserve a front-row seat
in my writing,
her presence merely a shadow
in the margins of my thoughts.

Now, she is definitely 'she/her,'
a distant memory,
and you,
you are the focus,
the one who truly matters.

I'll regret staying up until 2 a.m.
writing about you,
when the sun finds me
at 11 a.m.

The hours stretch thin,
yet here I am, wide awake,
as the world whispers to sleep,
chasing words that weave
the story of us.

But when morning light spills
through my window,
fatigue will settle in,
and I'll wonder if you
were worth the sacrifice
of dreams.

Yet for now, I'll linger
in the quiet hours,
crafting lines that trace
the contours of my heart,
knowing tomorrow's regret
will be another line
in our shared poem.

I've been falling,
hitting the ground,
rising high
and slamming back down
over and over and over again
for years.

Every descent felt like an end,
a reminder of gravity's grip,
each impact a familiar ache
etched into my bones,
my resilience tested
by the cycles of ascent and crash.

But this time, when I fell,
I came down softly,
landing on the pillows
you laid down
for me,

your love cushioning my descent,
turning chaos into calm,
transforming my spirals
into graceful arcs,
finding peace
in the gentleness of your embrace.

I've been so hyper-focused
on my own healing journey,
pouring energy into mending
the fractured pieces of myself,
lost in the labyrinth of self-repair,
each step a cautious venture
toward wholeness.

Yet it's taken her saying,
twice now,
that she doesn't want to get hurt,
her words echoing in my mind,
a gentle reminder that love
is a delicate balance,
a dance between giving and receiving,
where both hearts deserve
to be seen and safe.

Her quiet plea cuts through
my introspection,
a call to look beyond myself,
to nurture not just my own scars,
but to protect the tenderness
we are building,
to ensure that this path we walk
is a shared journey toward healing
for us both.

Self,
I am done with the lethargy,
the endless cycle of tiredness
that has kept me listless,
wandering in a haze of inertia.

I crave the mentality
that once drove me,
the fire that ignited my will
to do and achieve,
to transform ambition
into accomplishment.

Months of rest and mental healing
have been my refuge,
a necessary pause to mend,
but now it's time
to rise from the floor of contemplation,
to reclaim the energy
that once propelled me forward.

It's time to shake off the stagnation,
to reignite the spark within,
and to embrace the momentum
of "doing the damn thing."
No more delays,
no more waiting—
just action, purpose,
and the pursuit of what I know I can be.

We began our journey on Halloween Day,
a date that marks the start of something new,
and since then, the path has felt peculiar,
twisting in ways I struggle to articulate.

It's strange, this unfolding chapter,
a blend of desire and uncertainty,
where my wish to be her girlfriend
clashes with doubts that I may not be ready.

Or perhaps I am ready,
yet find myself in need of validation,
craving clarity in my feelings,
to understand what I want and need,
both from her and from life itself.

The journey is both thrilling and confusing,
a dance between readiness and hesitation,
as I navigate these emotions,
seeking guidance to reconcile
my heart's longing with the reality
of what lies ahead.

I wonder if, as she gazes at me,
her thoughts drift to the notion
that I might be lost in memories of you.

The truth is, I am.
In those quiet moments,
my mind wanders back to what was,
even as I stand here with her.

The echoes of you linger,
a subtle presence in the corners of my heart,
casting shadows even as I try to be present,
to fully embrace the now.

Kendra

She drifted down to me
like a light breeze,
gently shaking an oak leaf
from its branch
in mid-autumn—
quietly, with grace.

With her, she brought
the joy I cherish
in the smallest things:
natural laughter,
bottomless conversation,
settling softly in my ready hands.

I wrote a poem
about you last night.

This morning, you texted,
"Good morning, love."

By evening, you were gone,
your words fading into silence
eight hours later.

Now I must miss you
until the weight of your absence
is no longer heavy,
until the remnants of you
fade into distant memories,
softening into the corners of my mind,
where time slowly erases
the sharp edges of longing.

I will wait for the day
when the ache of your absence
becomes a gentle reminder,
no longer a constant burden,
until I am left only
with the quiet of moving on,
the peace of acceptance,
and the gentle rhythm
of new beginnings
where once there was only
the sound of your name.

I'm not eating,
not sleeping,
I'm functional, but only barely,
a shadow of my former self
moving through days
in a haze of existence,
struggling to hold on
to fragments of normalcy
while my body and mind
drift on the edge of exhaustion.

Each day is a tightrope
walked with weary steps,
my energy spent
on maintaining the facade
of being okay,
though inside I'm unraveling,
caught between the need to sustain
and the weight of just getting by.

It's minutes that stretch to hours,
hours that spiral into anxiety,
anxiety crystallizing into tears—

tears that transform moments
into shadows of laughter lost,
each drop a reminder
of what could have been
a chorus of joy now silent,
replaced by the quiet weight
of what I've missed.

You said,
"You check all the boxes,"
and it was, without a doubt,
the kindest thing I've been told
in three years.

Forgive me for believing you,
for letting those words weave
a fragile hope,
only to find it unraveling
in the cold light of truth.

You gave me happiness
I hadn't felt in three years,
a fleeting light that warmed
the corners of my heart.

Then, in just one week,
you took it away,
leaving behind shadows
where joy once danced.

The ones who keep walking away
are the ones who tell me
how amazing I am.

If I'm so incredible,
why do you keep leaving?
Your words paint me in light,
but your steps vanish into the dark.

When my phone vibrates,
a spark ignites within me,
as my soul leaps, hoping it's you.
I yearn for it to be you,
before I even check.

But it's not you,
and everything inside me
sinks,
drowning in the weight of unfulfilled hope.

Days drifted by,
your name absent from my screen,
mornings came and went
without a 'good morning' text,
numbers on the clock climbing,
then resetting,
day after endless day.

Other names flickered
in my notifications,
until at last,
there you were.

I opened it,
hoping for more,
only to find a laughing emoji
at my story.

I'm not going to tell you,
but I miss you.
I want to reach out –
call you now
to hear your voice,
to see that smile
I was falling in love with.

But I can't.
You ended us,
and I have to respect that boundary.

You were foolish to think we could ever
just be friends,
when I was falling in love with you.

Now I'm stuck,
like a book left open
on a blank page,
because we didn't finish our story.

Something scared you away,
and I'm left learning how
to close our book
unfinished.

Today, I heard your voice again
on Snapchat,
the first time in four days,
a distant reminder
of the voice I was falling for,
after ten hours of its melody
for six days unbroken.

The sound was bittersweet,
a soft sting of longing,
and I told you I missed you.

You replied with a cold,
"Why lol."

A sharp edge
of reality's blade.

In that simple phrase,
I found the closure I sought.

Thank you.

Don't inquire about the wedding dreams I hold
if you don't truly envision a future with me.
Don't ask for the details of our vows
if you can't see us in the years ahead.
For how can we plan the celebration
when the foundation of our togetherness
is still uncertain, wavering
on the edge of possibility?

I'm done writing about you.
The ink has dried on our seven days,
the fleeting moments of our 'talking stage.'
I have nothing more to say,
no lines left to pen
on the brief chapter we shared.
The words have exhausted their purpose,
and silence now speaks louder
than any verse I could craft.

Your texts are the only verses
that draw me from my pages,
the sole lines I'll set my book aside
to respond to.

In the quiet of my reading,
where words dance on the page,
it is your message
that punctuates my solitude,
a call that stirs me
from the inked embrace of fiction.

Each notification
is a sonnet I cannot ignore,
a verse I must answer,
for your text is the living prose
that interrupts my narrative,
turning my story's course
to meet yours.

I advise my friends
to ignore, block, and delete
their problems,
yet I keep you
on every social feed—

a testament to my own toxic trait.

While I preach the art of dismissal,
I cling to your presence,
perpetually entangled
in the threads of virtual connection.

My counsel is sound,
but my actions betray
the very wisdom I dispense.
In the realm of advice, I am resolute,
but in the landscape of my own life,
I am lost in contradiction.

I should delete you from Snap,
erase the trace of your presence
from my notifications.

Yet, there's a strange comfort
in seeing you as the first
to view my stories,
your name a familiar touch
in the sea of digital faces.

It's a small reassurance,
a reminder that you're still here,
even if only in the fleeting moments
between our silences.

So I linger in this paradox,
holding on to the fleeting echoes
of your attention,
while knowing I should let go.

You're not like my ex-wife,
who thrived on the back-and-forth
of text arguments,
the endless volley of words
that kept us tangled in discord.

With you, silence stretches,
days drift by without a reply,
a quiet void where words used to clash.
Your absence is a calm,
a stark contrast to the storm
of my past exchanges.

Brianna

and

Natalie

You're so sweet,
so irresistibly sweet,
your interest a tender warmth
in a place where I can't return it.

You're captivated by me,
while I'm entirely unmoved,
a reflection of disinterest
in the face of your affection.

I'm sorry for the dissonance,
for the chasm between your heart
and the coldness of my own.

It's a vexing irony –
your desire for me burns bright,
a relentless, undying flame.
Yet, as fervently as you want me,
I ache with equal intensity
for her.

Your longing mirrors my own,
a cruel symmetry
that only deepens the divide,
each wish unfulfilled
by the other's heart.

Why do I feel this weight
when affection blooms
in the midst of my healing?

I'm meant to be rising,
not sinking under the burden
of hearts drawn to
a faded reflection of me.

I should be mending,
not grappling with the sting
of being loved as a
watered-down version
of myself.

Their feelings, sincere yet misplaced,
only highlight the chasm
between who I am now
and who I wish to become.

I met you,
but the contours of your soul
are still a mystery to me,
and in these times,
knowing someone is a daunting journey.

Will I discover
you are still healing,
emotionally distant,
a soul not yet whole?

Will I find out
you're sharing your heart with others,
while I'm merely a stopgap
in your quest for something more?

Will my time with you
be another chapter of wasted moments,
a repeat of patterns
I've long hoped to escape?

Will our connection
flicker briefly,
only to be extinguished
by an unexplained departure?

Will we spend weeks
entangled in conversation,
only to clash irreparably
and sever all ties?

Will you become
a true partner,

a future I dare to envision,
moving in together, building dreams?

Will we fall into a love
that grows with each shared day,
constructing a life
filled with purpose and joy?

Or will I be left alone,
crying in the solitude of my bed,
haunted by the remnants
of past heartbreaks and disappointments?

Kayla

You don't give me butterflies.
I don't hover over my phone,
waiting for your next message.
I'm not drawn to endless chatter.

You're being you,
I'm being me.

Perhaps this is what normal
feels like…

Maybe…

Just maybe?

I dreamed of waking in the early hush
when dawn's light barely kissed the room,
a soft glow spilling across the space.

I turned and saw you beside me,
sleeping peacefully in the gentle light.
I rolled closer,
my arm finding its place around your waist,
and fell back into the warmth of dreams,
held by the quiet serenity of morning.

Where it was her in my dreams,
now it is you.
The spaces once filled with her essence
are now softly occupied by you,
as if the universe has shifted
to make room for your presence
in the landscape of my slumber.

It's been sixteen days since we first said hello.
I've etched the sound of your voice into my memory,
and now it plays on a loop in my mind,
whenever my heart aches with longing for you.
Each trace of your words
is a gentle reminder of the connection we share,
a melody of absence that only your presence
can truly soothe.

None of these poems
hold a candle
to the warmth you've brought me
since our first "good morning" text.
Their words pale
against the light of your kindness,
each line a mere shadow
to the brilliance of your presence.

You make me grasp what it means
when they say, "love is patient, love is kind."
In your presence, I see the truth
of patience woven into every moment,
and kindness reflected in each gesture.
You bring these concepts to life,
showing me the essence of love
in the most beautiful, tangible ways.

It brings me a joy as profound
as the stillness of dawn,
when the first light touches the earth
and reveals the hidden beauty
of the world waking anew.

This joy is the same as when I behold
a painting that stirs my soul,
or a sunrise that bathes the sky
in hues of gold and amber.

But it is in the simplicity of your smile
that I find a pure, unspoken grace,
a moment of serene delight
that mirrors the quiet splendor
I cherish in the most beautiful things.

Your smile,
a gentle curve that holds
the essence of all that is good,
offers me a peace
as deep and as true
as any beauty I've ever known.

Little did I know
the new year would unfold
a tapestry of peace
woven with threads of confidence
and ambition renewed.

In the midst of this fresh beginning,
you arrived,
a serendipitous gift,
adding your light
to the dawn of my new year.

Your presence
has become a part of the serenity
that colors my days,
a companion to the dreams
I now dare to chase.

I turn my text messages to you
into poems,
crafting each word
with the tenderness of ink on paper,
weaving our conversations
into verses and stanzas,
where every "good morning"
becomes a stanza of hope,
and each "goodnight"
a lullaby of longing.

In the space between our texts,
I find the rhythm of my heart,
and in the simplicity of your replies,
the muse for every line
I pen in your name.

You are both the subject and the inspiration,
the refrain of my verses,
and the silent partner
in this poetic dance
of our exchanged words.

Every 'good morning' is a prelude
to the next chapter of you I'm about to discover,
an unveiling of new facets,
each day a step closer
to the deeper layers of your being
that will enrich my journey.
Each greeting is a promise
of the evolving story
we write together,
with each dawn revealing
a new dimension of who you are.

You said hello,
and two months later, I responded with my own.

Had I answered your greeting
when it first reached me,
perhaps we would have spiraled into chaos,
for I was not yet ready.

The universe, with its intricate design,
must have had its reasons
for timing my response as it did.

In its wisdom,
it orchestrated our encounter
when I was prepared,
ensuring our meeting came with purpose
and clarity.

You're still a stranger,
a new presence in the vast expanse
of my life's tapestry.

Yet deep within,
in the most remote corners
of my soul's hidden recesses,
I sense a quiet certainty
that I am destined to love you.

It's a whisper from the depths,
a truth unspoken,
but firmly rooted in the fabric of my being,
foretelling a connection
that transcends our present unfamiliarity.

Meeting you has been like the sound of soft piano music,
playing in the background of a cozy café,
while I sit in a corner booth,
reading poetry and sipping on coffee.

It's a gentle, soothing melody
that weaves through the air,
a harmonious backdrop
to the quiet moments of reflection
and the comforting warmth of a well-loved ritual.

Your presence is the subtle tune
that adds depth to my ordinary moments,
a symphony of connection
that turns simple experiences
into cherished memories.

I've never met you in person,
yet right now, I miss you
with a depth that feels like a murmur
from a past life.

It's as if our souls have crossed paths
in some distant memory,
where moments spent together
linger like an unspoken promise,
etched into the fabric of time.

This longing feels ancient,
a connection woven through the ages,
binding us in a way that defies
the logic of our present selves.

Violet,

how tranquil my life has become
since the storm of you
has faded into absence,
leaving behind a serene calm
where once there was turbulence.

I wonder how long and how tight the hug will be when
we finally meet.
I wonder if I'll be able to let go, or if I'll linger, unable
to step away.
I wonder what it will feel like to hold your hand, to
intertwine our fingers.
Will I be shy, lost in silence, or will nerves make me
chatter incessantly?
I wonder if I'll become addicted to the scent of your
skin,
if cuddling with you will feel like finding a place where
my soul can finally rest.
What if I cry when you leave,
or if it physically pains my heart to watch you walk
away?
But what if I know, deep down, that you'll return?
What if we fall in love, and you choose me?
What if you're everything I've ever wanted and needed,
and I am the same for you?

-Your babe?

In just 19 days,
I've come to a truth
I wish to share with you:

I love you.

I don't love you—
not yet.

I like you a whole lot,
and I'm drawn to the word
love.

I don't love you yet,
but when the urge to say
'I love you'
rises,

I run to my journal,
where I craft a poem
about you instead.

Our words flow too smoothly,
like a river untroubled by stones.
I wonder if this ease
hides unseen depths.

Is it a red flag
when talking feels too easy,
when vulnerability offers itself
as if we've known each other
for lifetimes instead of days?

Does the comfort mask
what we choose not to see,
like a calm before a storm
or a wave poised to crash?

Is there a truth we overlook
in words unguarded and free,
whispering caution
between our lines?

I question if this ease
is a warning to tread carefully,
as we walk this path
that feels like déjà vu.

It's so hard not to just
read you all the poetry
I've penned in your name,
to let each verse spill out
and show you the depths
of how I really feel.

The words are a river
that runs deep within me,
yearning to flow towards you,
to lay bare the emotions
that linger in each stanza,
each carefully chosen line.

But for now,
they remain inked in my pages,
a private testament
to what you mean to me,
until the moment I can share
my heart's poetry with you.

I shared a poem on Snapchat,
and I bet many of you
thought it was about you—

It's not.
It's about her,
the 'her' I converse with daily,
since I stopped responding to you.

The verses were meant
for a different chapter,
a new rhythm I'm learning,
while your name fades
into the margins of my past.

Sometimes I imagine
your fingertips,
a gentle touch,
drifting through my hair—
a caress that stirs
the depths of my soul,
where warmth and longing
intertwine.

I write your name,
then place a comma,
as if that pause
holds the key
to how I might
confess
that I may be
falling in love
with you.

You keep telling me
I'm beautiful,
and I find it hard
to believe your words
from someone whose smile
shines as brightly
as yours.

You're on Facetime,
drifting into sleep,
while I'm falling
deeper into love.

You said you could never get tired
of looking at me,
and I replied with a cautious smile,
"Be careful...
you're weaving words
that might catch me
in a web of feelings."

Your gaze, a gentle promise,
spun threads of emotion
I'm now entangled in—
a delicate dance of desire
and unspoken hopes.

I hope that talk of desire
doesn't overshadow
the deeper conversations
we share—
the dreams we weave,
the hopes we nurture,
the goals we strive toward,
the fears we confront,
and your boundless love
for your mother.

May our dialogues
remain rich and meaningful,
uninterrupted by fleeting moments,
grounded in the essence
of who we are and wish to be.

I'm humming
melodies that stir
a sense of joy
I haven't felt in ages,
a gentle reminder
that happiness
has returned
to my heart.

We are still strangers,
yet I've glimpsed your most intimate moments,
a canvas of vulnerability laid bare.
But the shadows lurking deep within your soul,
the demons yet unnamed,
remain a mystery to me,
hidden in the depths
where our paths have yet to tread.

You're likely to discover the layers of me,
unravel my essence,
and in time,
grow weary,
and leave.

Meanwhile,
I'll stick to my routines—
the gym, the work,
the daily grind.

Maybe I'll cry,
or perhaps erase this later,
a fleeting moment of raw truth
etched in transient ink.

You discouraged me,
undermined all we'd built
over the last twenty days.

In my moments of vulnerability,
when I reached out,
you met me with laughter,
hinting that our conversations
might end.

I'm not in love with you,
just tangled in the realm of feelings—
where you reside
between mere interest
and something deeper,
a space where you occupy
the delicate space
between a passing fancy
and a lover's embrace.

I call you "baby" now,
sometimes "babe,"
a testament to how my heart
has opened up.

I was ready to.

You've been saying "te quiero"
for a few days,
soft syllables wrapped
in tender intent.

I know what "I love you"
is in Spanish,
but I keep it unspoken,
a quiet understanding
between us.

In your words,
I sense the undercurrent
of deeper feelings,
a silent admission
I'm content to leave
in the realm of mystery.

You said "I love you"
first,
without queries
or the weight of expectation
for me to mirror your sentiment.

In that unguarded moment,
I see the truth of your heart,
a testament to the depth
of what you feel.

It's clear now –
you love me.

Violet,
I want to write about you—

It's been three days
since you left my apartment,
three days since our first weekend
woven into time's fabric.

Three days,
and still, I struggle
to find the words
to capture what transpired
in my heart
and in these sheets.

The moments linger,
unspoken and profound,
leaving me with a silence
that speaks volumes
about the weight
of what we shared.

You showed up at 11 PM
after an eight-hour drive,
a testament to your unwavering resolve.

"Tell me you're a lesbian
without telling me you're a lesbian,"
you said,
and in that moment,
every mile traveled
spoke louder than words ever could.

I don't care what fills our hours,
as long as I'm given more time
to witness your smile,
to listen to your laughter.

Every moment with you
becomes a cherished chapter,
a line written in the story of us.

Twice now, I've tried to write
how I feel about you,
only to scribble it all out,

because the feelings I have
scramble my thoughts,
making it impossible
to translate them into words
and capture them on paper.

Each attempt ends
with lines crossed out,
ink blurred by emotion,
leaving a mess of hopes
and unspoken truths.

The chaos in my heart
resists definition,
a whirlwind of sentiments
too vast to contain
in the confines of a page.

But maybe this confusion
speaks for itself,
a testament to the depth
of what I feel for you,
a poem in its own right.

For weeks, I spun the story
of being the victim in my mind,
letting darkness murmur doubt.

But I'm over it now.

The foundation of us is solid,
no room left for excuses
or the comfort of old patterns.

I've reached the summit,
tired of the weight I carried,
and now, I let it go—
ready to move forward,
clear-headed and free.

Did you see me as the enemy
as we began to unravel each other?
It felt that way—
a constant undercurrent of suspicion
tinged every exchange.

You spoke with bold confidence,
asserting your worth,
declaring that if we parted ways,
you'd be just fine,
for you've spent a year alone,
healing and knowing precisely
what you seek in a woman.

Strange, isn't it?
How someone who claims to be 'healed'
could end a relationship they once cherished,
overwhelmed by emotions
they couldn't articulate,
only to retract their words
and beg for another chance.

'Healed,' you say?
Isn't it peculiar?

My lungs forgot to inhale
when you squeezed my hand
and whispered,
"You're a really good person."

Your words were like a gentle tide,
pushing me to the shore of a quiet moment,
where breath caught in a still,
unexpected embrace.

In that simple gesture,
the world held its breath,
and in your affirmation,
I found a space where I was simply seen.

Seeing your smile
was like taking an overdose
of the most potent drug,
letting myself drift
into a blissful oblivion,
where every worry vanished
in the pure, intoxicating light
of your gaze.

You were never mine—
just a love on lease
for sixty-seven days,

a fleeting ember
that warmed my heart,
but flickered and faded,

leaving behind a memory
of borrowed moments
and a love that wasn't meant
to stay.

Remember when you said,
"I'll never let go again"?

A promise I embraced,
a lie I believed,
woven into the fabric
of our shared moments,
each thread a hope
tangled with dreams.

You spoke with certainty,
as if your words
were the very anchor
that would hold us
against the tides.

But beneath the surface,
the truth unraveled,
revealing a chasm
where trust once bridged
the distance between us.

In every reassurance you gave,
a subtle doubt lingered,
and I held on
to the fragile illusion,
until it frayed,
leaving behind the remnants
of what I wished was true.

Now, in the silence
where promises have faded,
I find myself untangling
the reverberations of your vow,
a lesson learned
in the delicate art of letting go.

My anxiety
keeps me in a constant state
of unease,
haunted by the fear
that you might leave.

Despite every assurance
you offer,
I'm still gripped
by the dread
that at any moment,
you'll change your mind.

You love me,
and yet I grapple with the thought
that you might find a reason
to walk away by the end of the day,
or with the dawn's first light.

In your gaze, there's a tenderness,
but an undercurrent of doubt lingers,
haunting the edges of our moments,
murmuring fears of an inevitable parting.

Each day, I cling to the fragile hope
that love will anchor you,
but I tremble at the thought
that the very love that holds us
might unravel,
thread by delicate thread,
with the rise of each new sun.

Your words offer comfort,
yet my heart remains restless,
caught in a dance of longing
and anxious anticipation.

In every embrace, I search
for the reassurance I crave,
but the fear persists,
that the day might come
when your love is a memory
held in the light of yesterday.

And when I'm scraping my fingers,
desperate to climb out of life's deep pit,
tears blurring my vision,
sore fingers clawing at the sides,

when at last I reach the top,
expecting a hand to pull me up,
I find only emptiness—
the ones who cheered me on have vanished.

In the silence, I am abandoned once more,
my last ounce of strength depleted,
and I slide back down,
whimpering,
to the depths from which I fought to escape.

Abandoned again.

Sometimes I want to tell you I miss you,
because the ache inside me is real and persistent,
but I hold back,
afraid to cause you pain with my confession,
afraid that knowing my heart yearns for you
might bring a hurt
that lingers longer than the distance between us.

The more she pressed me to conform,
the tighter her grip, the more I slipped away,
a balloon set adrift in the wind,
drifting further from the ground
where I once stood firm.

Her expectations, like heavy chains,
only loosened my tether,
and I floated, untethered and free,
lost in the vast expanse of who I am meant to be.

I find myself lost in thoughts of solitude,
dreaming of the quiet that once was mine,
where silence reigned and space was abundant,
a blank canvas where I could paint my peace.

The reverberations of my own voice,
the stillness of empty rooms,
beckon me with their serene embrace,
offering a retreat from the tangled web
of shared existence and constant connection.

I ponder the solace in solitude,
the freedom in being alone again,
where every corner of my life
is a reflection of my own choosing,
unshaped by the presence of another.

Violet,
I sent her songs
that once played for you,
melodies that carried
traces of what was,
notes that linger
on the edges of memory.

That moment on the couch,
after we both felt the burst of inner ecstasy,
our eyes met, and for an instant,
I sensed our souls intertwine.

I didn't want to say this,
but I needed you
to help me get over my ex.
I'm truly sorry I let you fall
for a version of me that wasn't real,
just a guise to move on from her.

You wanted to talk about my ex,
to draw lines in the sand,
to be everything she was not,
as if your worth was defined
by what you weren't.

In your quest to differentiate,
you lost sight of who you were—
a person already complete,
whole and shining in your own light.

Instead of embracing your truth,
you sculpted yourself around her shadow,
as if becoming her opposite
would reveal the best of you.

Yet the person you needed to be
was never hidden in contrast,
but in the quiet strength
of being simply yourself.

I don't even know what a healthy love
looks like at this point.
The lines blur, the definitions fade,
and I search through fragments of broken promises
for a shape I can't quite grasp.

In the maze of past hurt and failed attempts,
the image of love is distorted,
a mirage lost in a desert of confusion,
where the oasis of genuine affection
seems just beyond reach.

I wander through the halls of what I've known,
trying to piece together a mosaic
of what love should be,
but each shattered piece
reflects a different story,
a different shade of longing.

What does it mean to love
without the shadows of old wounds?
What does it look like
when trust and warmth
are not just fleeting moments
but the steady pulse of a shared life?

At this point, I only know
the vast expanse of my uncertainty,
the quest for a love that is more than
a series of lessons learned the hard way—
a love that is whole, clear,
and true.

The more you chose your ex over me,
the more I found myself wanting
to mirror her,
to step into the mold
she once occupied,
to become a reflection of her
in your eyes.

In your preference,
I saw a shadow of my own
doubt and desire,
a longing to reshape myself
into the version
that might hold your gaze,
might be worthy of your choice.

Yet in the struggle to become
what you seemed to want,
I lost sight of the person
I was striving to be—
a distorted image
crafted from fragments
of someone else's past.

The more I learned who I was,
the clearer it became
that you are lost
in the fog of your own identity,
wandering through
a haze of uncertainty
where your reflection
remains blurred and distant.

In my journey to self-discovery,
your lack of self-awareness
stood out like a silent void,
a mirror unpolished,
revealing not my image,
but the emptiness
that lingers in your own soul.

I wanted us to heal in tandem,
to mend our wounds side by side,
two broken souls finding solace
in each other's embrace.

I envisioned our hearts
becoming whole together,
each step a shared journey
toward understanding and renewal,
where our scars would blend
into a tapestry of recovery,
woven by the threads of mutual support.

It wasn't until the fourth goodbye
in just three months' time
that clarity struck—
how deeply I craved solitude again.

The solitude, once a quiet ache,
now feels like a balm,
a reprieve from the erratic dance
of a love that couldn't hold steady.

Being alone brings a peace
unseen in the turbulence of us,
where inconsistency fades
into a steady rhythm of my own making.

I've reached a place where I'm content
with the quiet solitude of solo outings,
where the cinema becomes my retreat,
and I find solace in the dark,
savoring the flicker of stories
without the need for company.

In the comfort of my own presence,
I've learned to embrace the peace
that comes with enjoying the simple joy
of a movie alone,
where the screen's glow
becomes a companion of its own.

And my soul fell deeper in love
when you reached out,
asking how you could help
with the weight of my anxiety,
your concern a gentle bridge
over the chasm of my fears.

In that moment, your care
wove itself into the fabric of my heart,
each word a tender thread
binding us closer,
as you offered your presence
to ease the shadows that lingered.

I wonder if I'm stringing you along,
torn between the threads of lingering love
and the simple pleasure of knowing
you yearn for my attention.

Is it the comfort of familiar warmth
that keeps me tethered to this dance,
or the thrill of having you chase
a fleeting shadow of what we once were?

In the quiet moments,
I question if my heart truly knows
where it stands,
or if it's merely caught
in the pull of a bittersweet game.

I don't think I cared
whether I truly liked or loved you.

I needed someone to share the weight,
to help with the bills and the burdens
that come with living.

In the practicalities of life,
your presence was a solution,
a temporary balm for the everyday struggles
more than a connection of hearts.

The necessity of companionship
outweighed the search for affection,
as I sought relief in the steadiness
of shared responsibilities.

I never claimed to be normal,
you just fell for the mask I wore,
the façade I crafted
to hide the chaos within.

Behind the carefully painted smile
and the practiced gestures,
you saw only the surface,
mistaking it for the truth.

The mask was a shield,
a veil that concealed the storm,
and you embraced the illusion,
believing it was the whole of me.

I know I'm damaged,
and so are you.

The difference lies
in the path I've chosen—
seeking therapy
and medication,
trying to mend the cracks
with professional care.

You, too, carry wounds,
but haven't walked the same road,
haven't reached for the tools
I've embraced to heal.

We're both fractured,
but the ways we cope
show the divide
in our journeys towards wholeness.

If you're not in therapy,
seeking self-awareness
of your shortcomings,
then don't bother
trying to shoot your shot with me.

I need more than words
and promises;
I need someone
actively working
on their own growth,
someone who understands
the value of introspection.

Without that effort,
don't waste your time—
I'm not here for
a superficial connection
but for someone
who strives to better themselves
from within.

How do ordinary lives unfold
if not in the throes of extreme highs and lows?
Is there a steady rhythm,
a balanced pulse
that guides their days
through the mundane and the serene?

Do they navigate existence
with a calm that eludes the rest,
where joy and sorrow
coalesce into a seamless dance,
uninterrupted by the peaks
and valleys of emotional extremes?

I wonder if their hearts beat
to a different cadence,
where stability
is the norm,
and the wild fluctuations
of passion and despair
are but distant remnants,
replaced by the quiet hum
of the everyday.

I knew something was amiss
when the soul within me
became a stranger,
its once familiar contours
lost in the shifting sands
of an uncharted self.

Why do I feel so detached from my own existence,
drifting in the chasm between self and reality?
Why do my thoughts seem so intangible,
while the world around me remains so solid, so real?

Why do I question how my body persists in its rhythm,
while my mind unravels and disintegrates,
caught in the spiral of its own self-destruction?

I wish you knew I'm not waiting for you,
though it might seem that way.
We're not together,
and I've found myself
in conversation with someone else.
It's a reality you might not see,
but I'm moving forward,
not anchored in yesterday's promise.

You grew upset
because I withheld
fragments of my past.

But I do not owe you
any of that history.

It's mine to reveal
at my own pace,
to those I choose.

I don't owe you
that information.

I step out onto the pavement
and begin a light jog,
my ponytail swaying
with each easy stride.

But I'm not really running;
I'm seated on your couch,
cross-legged, the movie paused.
In my mind, I jog through a scene,
while you watch me, a silent observer.

I say nothing,
as everything within me
shuts down, and autopilot takes over.
I see myself in slow motion,
each step a quiet defiance.

You sit there, the TV's glow
painting your face,
disgust curling in your voice.

"You're not my person."
"I don't want to be with you."
"I'm not happy."

And there I am,
one foot in front of the other,
running, running, running—
coping, coping, coping.

I wanted to cry,
to kick and scream,
to crumble at your feet
and plead for your love,
begging for another chance.

But then I saw what you were losing—
not what I was losing.
I remembered my worth,
and chose to depart with grace,
with dignity intact.

I set 'home' into my GPS
and drove away from
the wreckage you left behind.

Love, it should not have been that hard—
a gentle journey,
not a battleground.
It was meant to flow
like a quiet stream,
not surge with storms
and tangled currents.

What we had
should have been effortless,
a dance in soft rhythms,
not a struggle
to stay afloat.
Love, it should not have been that hard.

I am a hurricane,
a tempest of chaos.
If you take my hand,
I won't let go—
not through the storm's fury,
nor the calm that follows.

I am a whirlwind,
unpredictable and fierce,
binding us together
in the eye of the gale,
where the world spins wildly
and silence speaks volumes.

You were supposed to send me flowers
when I was still yours—
not after you broke my heart,
sending me on an eight-hour drive home,
crying on the phone to my friends.

They are beautiful blooms,
but they only serve to remind me
of that lonely drive,
not of the love you once promised.

You were breaking up with me for the third time,
and I felt I should have been crying,
but no tears came. Instead,
everything turned icy and cold.

My heart went stiff,
my lips curved into a snarl.
How dare you toy with my love again,
after more chances than you deserved?

My faith and trust in you
became a source of disgust.
I should have been crying,
but my body knew better—

no tears to waste on you anymore,
only a frozen resolve,
a heart hardened by your betrayal,
and a quiet determination to move on.

The longer you stood silent,
letting me slip away,
the easier it became
to walk out the door.

Your lack of effort
made each step lighter,
each moment of departure
a little less heavy.

With every breath you didn't take,
every word you left unspoken,
the distance grew smaller
between me and the exit.

Your indifference
greased the path of my leaving,
turning what should have been
a struggle into a mere stroll.

I don't miss you.
I text that I do,
but the words are empty reflections,
reflections that deceive more than they reveal.

The truth is shrouded in the pretense
of longing I fabricate,
a script I recite to mask
the reality of my indifference.

Why do I play this game,
this dance of deceit?
Perhaps I seek the thrill
of a truth left unspoken.

One day, you'll unravel the lie,
discover the hollow declarations
hidden behind the curtain of my words,
and then, when you see through the façade,
it will be then that I break your heart.

I don't love the same way.
I want to apologize for that,
but it's your fault we are here.

I still say, "I love you,"
but it's mostly because
you find comfort in hearing it.
My words are shadows
of what you seek,
cast by the light
of your own expectations.

I'd be lying if I said
I saw a future with you.
Deep down, I knew we were
a dumpster waiting to ignite,
a blaze waiting to happen.

Our paths were strewn
with the remnants of regret,
and the sparks of discord
were too bright to ignore.

I don't know if it's the Sagittarius fire,
or the remnants of PTSD and anxiety,
or the relentless cycle of heartbreak
that has shaped me,

but I no longer care if you unravel
the reasons behind my indifference.
I don't love you like I did
after you broke my heart again.

Why does this absence of empathy
for someone who wounded me
make me feel like a villain?
Is it the coldness of self-preservation
that tarnishes my own reflection?

You broke things off again,
but this time, you spoke of a tattoo—
my name etched on your chest.
Your love bombing spirals,
a wild storm of promises
that drowns out the truth.

You fracture our connection,
yet offer inked declarations,
your words a paradox,
a tempest of affection
that overshadows the silence
of a love already lost.

You said you'd ask me every day
to be your girlfriend
until I said yes,
a ritual of devotion
or stubborn pursuit.

I'm caught between flattered
by your unyielding chase,
and repelled
by the weight of your relentlessness.

Your persistence paints a picture,
but I wonder if it's
a canvas of romance
or a mirror reflecting
a boundary crossed.

The closer you press into my space,
the more your presence turns to distance.
Each step you take toward me
further fuels my aversion,
as if your attempts to bridge the gap
only widen it in my eyes.

I've been adrift,
lost in the haze of what comes next,
instead of savoring the pulse of now.
My mind drifts forward,
while the present slips quietly away,
unnoticed, uncelebrated.

I oscillate between shadows and light,
torn between the ache of solitude
and the solace it offers.

One moment, loneliness wraps around me
like a shroud of melancholy,
weighing heavy on my heart.

The next, solitude's silence
whispers gratitude,
a quiet refuge from the chaos.

In this pendulum swing,
I seek balance
between despair and contentment,
finding peace in the ebb and flow.

I find myself adrift,
boredom's grasp tightens,
with no voice to call upon
to chase away the dullness.

I linger in idle spaces,
while responsibilities wait,
a quiet rebellion against the tasks
that I know I should be embracing.

In the emptiness of silence,
the absence of company
turns the mundane into a void,
a distraction from the duties
that beckon from the periphery.

I'll find a thousand distractions,
each one more compelling than the last,
skirting the edges of responsibility
with fervent dedication.

The tasks I should embrace
are overshadowed by diversions,
each moment spent evading
what I know must be done.

In the maze of avoidance,
I navigate with practiced ease,
forsaking the essential
for the comfort of the trivial.

The more it beckons with necessity,
the more I shy away from its grasp.
Tasks loom like shadows,
each one a call to action I resist.

The weight of obligation
makes avoidance a refuge,
where procrastination
becomes a familiar companion.

She was a narcissistic manipulator,
a maestro of deceit and grand illusion,
but you? You wore your manipulations
with a subtler touch,
so I missed the signs in the beginning.

Your tactics were veiled,
an artful dance of influence and charm,
disguised in the guise of ordinary gestures,
unlike the overt theatricality I had known.

It took time to see through the facade,
to recognize the patterns you wove,
and by then, the subtlety had ensnared me,
leaving me tangled in the threads
of your quiet manipulation.

The longer I get to know you,
the more ashamed I am
of myself for not seeing
that you were merely mirroring me.

I didn't fall in love with you;
I fell in love with the version
of myself you were playing,
a reflection I mistook for true affection.

You mirrored my desires,
my hopes, and my dreams,
crafting a version of me
that I embraced as love.

In the end, it was not you I loved,
but the resonance of my own heart
dressed in your guise,
deceiving me with its familiar beat.

I should block you on everything—
clear the channels of your influence,
but I'm caught in the flicker
of your mind games,
finding a twisted amusement
in your manipulations.

Each message, each move,
a dance of mental chess
that I should ignore,
yet I linger,
curious about the next gambit,
entertained by the spectacle
of your elaborate charades.

I feel like a terrible person,
repeating 'I love you'
when the truth is
I never loved you at all.

Each 'I love you'
was a rehearsed line,
a response to a script
I never truly believed.

It's a hollow resonance
of something I didn't feel,
a facade I wore
to pacify a moment,
while inside,
the truth remained silent,
unspoken, and unfeeling.

You wasted the first four months
of what was meant to be
MY YEAR.

I want to blame you,
but I take full responsibility
for letting you squander my time,
for permitting the moments to slip away
under your watch.

The responsibility is mine
for allowing the days to drift
in the currents of your influence,
for sacrificing my own time
on the altar of our misaligned paths.

I don't want to talk to you anymore,
but with my history of abandonment issues,
I find myself paralyzed,
unsure of how to leave.

The very act of departure
feels like a foreign land,
a landscape I've yet to navigate,
where my own fears map out
the paths I can't seem to follow.

I'm caught between wanting to go
and the terror of leaving,
stuck in the limbo of knowing
I should walk away,
but not knowing how to sever
the ties that bind me,
how to escape
without feeling lost in the void.

I could tolerate you for survival,
navigating the space between us
as a means to an end,
a necessary endurance
to get through each day.

Yet love was a different realm,
a land I couldn't map out with you,
a territory where my heart
couldn't find its footing.

I could adapt to coexist,
find comfort in the compromise,
but to love you was a horizon
I could never reach,
a distant shore
my heart was never meant to touch.

The more I write about how I can't stand you,
the deeper the chasm between truth and words,
where each line penned
reveals the depth of my distaste,
yet I still find myself
whispering 'I love you'
through clenched teeth.

The disconnect grows wider,
a rift between what I feel
and what I say,
leaving me tangled in a web
of false declarations
and regret.

I want to let go,
to untangle the threads
of this exhausting experience,
but the thought of loneliness
after release grips me tight,
like a specter cast
by the weight of parting.

I fear the emptiness
that will follow
as I release us both,
the void that looms
where once was tangled connection,
leaving me to navigate
the quiet aftermath
of solitude and separation.

I'm waiting for your consistency,
even though you've shown me
for four months now
that it's a distant dream.

Why do I cling to the hope
that you'll change,
when each day has revealed
your inability to be steadfast?

Why am I stringing us both along,
trapped in a cycle
of false expectations
and repeated disappointments?

I've been talking to someone new
for a week now,
while you've been love bombing me
in a desperate bid to win me back.

I've been waiting for you to figure it out,
to see through the façade of my silence,
because I lack the nerve to tell you
that everything about you
makes my skin crawl.

Your attempts to rekindle
are met with a cold indifference,
as I silently distance myself,
hoping you'll understand
without me having to reveal
the depth of my discomfort.

Natasha

If you're wondering
if I'm writing about you,

I am.

Every line,
every verse,
captures the truth
I struggle to voice.

So yes,
each word
is a reflection
of the thoughts
I can't escape,
the emotions
I can't conceal.

You said you were content
with your life and who you are,
that my discontent
was a reflection of me,
not of you.

You placed the blame
on my unhappiness,
as if my struggle
to reconcile with myself
was the root of our discord,
ignoring how your satisfaction
didn't soothe
the unrest in my heart.

I relished your confession of self-love,
a truth you wore so proudly,
and I think you noticed it
in the subtle shift of my gaze.

You met my eyes with unflinching clarity
and spoke the words I feared,
"You don't love yourself."

My heart dropped at the revelation,
a dark secret laid bare,
exposed by the mirror of your honesty.
In that moment,
the depth of my own shadows
was declared out loud,
leaving me bare and vulnerable.

You confront me with my fears and insecurities,
forcing me to face the demons
I'd rather keep hidden.
You challenge me, not to amplify my doubts,
but to confront them head-on.

I'm torn between pushing you away
for imposing this uncomfortable growth
or holding you close
to cling to the attachment
that promises to unravel
when you inevitably walk away.

Caught in this whirlwind of emotions,
I struggle with the pull of closeness
against the fear of abandonment,
wondering if the comfort of your presence
is worth the chaos it might bring.

I feel like I share everything with you,
revealing my thoughts and secrets,
because there's a common thread
we both feel,
an unspoken connection
that binds us in understanding.

It's as if our souls recognize
a shared rhythm,
a mutual understanding
that draws out my confessions
and makes me vulnerable,
knowing that you, too, grasp
the essence of what we both experience.

When we hang out,
my guard melts away,
as if I've known you
since childhood,
as if our connection
spans across lifetimes,
etched in the traces
of another existence.

In your presence,
I feel a timeless ease,
as if we've shared
countless moments before,
our souls reunited
in this fleeting moment,
blurring the lines of past and present.

I don't want to make love to you
with my body;
I want to sit across a coffee shop table,
memorize the intricate details
in the iris of your eyes,
and feel love vibrate
back and forth
between us.

You're in like with me,
but if you fall in love
before you see me fall to my feet
in self-loathing,
regret,
sadness,

do you have the patience and compassion
to sit down next to me and just
be?

Just be... next to me.
Don't pick me up, don't coddle me.
Just be...

Because I will fall hard,
but I need to rise on my own,
always.

And that is what I need
from someone who loves me.

I'll never utter the words I spoke
while in love with you
to anyone else.

Those sentiments,
tender and raw,
were yours alone,
woven into the essence
of our shared moments.

No other heart will hear
the remnants of our language,
for those phrases belong
to a chapter closed,
etched in the history
of our singular connection.

Being overly questioned
triggers my PTSD,
a cascade of unease
flooding my mind,
each query a sharp reminder
of past wounds.

In the flood of interrogation,
I find myself adrift,
struggling to shield
my fragile peace
from the relentless tide
of intrusive curiosity.

Because of the PTSD from enduring
an abusive relationship
with a narcissist,

my phone remains silent,
notifications turned off,
an invisible barrier
against the echoes of intrusion.

I cannot trust the compliments
that come my way,
for I was never good enough,
no matter how hard I tried.

Each praise feels like a hollow reflection,
a soft deceit that I can't embrace,
because every effort I made
was met with silent disapproval,
every success tainted by doubt.

I was trained to doubt
the sincerity of affection,
to question the value of every kind word,
for in a world where nothing was ever enough,
even the sweetest of praises
were veiled in uncertainty.

I guard my heart against the flattery,
shielding it from the shards of false hope,
knowing that in the eyes of those
who have loved me with conditions,
no amount of praise
can ever be fully trusted.

Linking lips
and swaying hips,
blue eyes
meeting my green eyes.
An aurora of hazel
mixes between us—
are we adrift,
both aware and lost?

Violet,
I can't even conjure your face
in my mind anymore. Where once
I'd think of you alone,
doing the things you used to do,
your image has faded.

I look down in my imagination,
and all I see is a blur,
a remnant of what was once vivid.
Where you used to occupy space,
I find myself unable to move,
needing someone newer
to fill the void.

I don't find excuses to touch you;
it comes naturally in conversation,
yet every contact ignites
an electric current through my soul,
a jolt that sparks deep within
each time our skin connects.

I hope you find the strength to heal
from the emotional triggers that haunt you,
for I know the journey is arduous—
one I walk daily, too.

It's not the people who unsettle our peace,
but the remnants of past experiences,
etched deep, crafting our triggers,
hidden beneath layers of old pain.

I don't bring you unhappiness;
it's the weight of your history
that surfaces, reshaping our moments,
filling them with discontent.

Your struggle lies not just with me,
but with patience for yourself—
the time needed to unravel
the tangled threads of what causes you strife.

May you discover solitude and joy
in the quiet spaces of your own heart,
find the solace you seek
when you are alone, yet whole.

I wish you the best on your path,
where healing and happiness can blend,
and may you find the peace
that eluded us in the end.

It's as if we're bound by a secret pact,
a hidden club only we know the password to.
No one else grasps our private jokes,
or deciphers the handshakes we share.

Just the two of us, members of this clandestine union,
creating pacts and burying memories
in unmarked spots, deep within our hearts,
where only we can find them.

In this private realm, we carve our own symbols,
whispering secrets only we understand,
sealed in the quiet spaces of our shared moments,
etched in the silent ground of our connection.

Saying hello comes easily to you,
a grace that flows without effort.
But saying goodbye,
I've seen you falter,
a disquiet I've never witnessed before.

It's in those final moments
that your ease evaporates,
leaving a clumsy silence
where words once danced.
Goodbye wraps you in unease,
a discomfort stark against your usual ease,
revealing the fragility of farewells
beneath the veneer of your calm.

I've been conversing with others,
yet it's you who lingers,
always in the corner of my mind,
a master at appearing occupied,
though your sole aim is to stay,
reminding me of your presence,
anchored firmly in my thoughts.

Your subtle stance,
a professional illusion,
disguises the truth of your intent—
to remain there, persistent,
a shadow of yourself
in the corridors of my head,
refusing to fade away.

When I look at your hands,
I envision the countless women
who have felt your touch,
each gesture a testament to affection.
Your eyes, too, have beheld
the beauty of women,
reflecting adoration and warmth.

I don't feel envy;
I feel admiration.
I honor how you've used
both hands and gaze
to bestow kindness and love,
making others feel profoundly cherished.

After each heartbreak,
my eyes grow brighter,
as if each sorrow
adds a new brilliance.

Through all this time,
they have been illuminating,
radiating a light born
from the trials and tears,
shining with the resilience
of a heart that endures.

Take my hand and follow behind me
as I lead you down a path paved
with my oldest secrets.

Each step reveals the stories
carved into the cobblestones of time,
hidden truths and softly spoken words,
illuminated by the light of trust.

Together, we'll walk through the corridors
of my past, where memories linger,
and find solace in the understanding
of the roads I've traveled.

I already sense that when we finally share that space
together,
it will be extraordinary.
So, I'm not rushing toward it,
because I believe that the act itself
might overshadow our journey of understanding.

The anticipation of that moment
could become our main focus,
diverting attention from truly knowing each other
on a deeper, more meaningful level.

I'd rather savor the process,
discovering the essence of who we are
and how we connect,
before we let the physical experience
define our bond.

Being around you feels like returning
to a place I've longed for,
a sanctuary after a journey's end.
It's the warmth of familiar walls,
the comfort of a well-worn path,
where every moment spent apart
is softened by the ease of reunion.

You are the homecoming I didn't realize
I was yearning for,
the quiet refuge that soothes
the ache of distance and time.

I did it.
I got better.
I learned to choose me.
To love me.

I fought through tears,
doubt,
insecurities,
suicidal thoughts...
not once did I give up.

Each day I woke up
and tried again.
I stumbled,
but kept going.

The hardest thing I've ever done
was choosing myself.

Now I laugh tears of joy
that I did it.
I got better.
I learned to choose me,
to love me,
every day.

I think back to the version of me
that existed five months ago,
and all I remember is a stranger.
I don't know her anymore.

All the growth and healing
have reshaped my reflection,
leaving me unable to recall
the me who made all those poor decisions.

She is a figure, fading
in the light of newfound strength,
a distant memory in the halls of my mind,
eclipsed by the person I've become.

I've shed that skin,
emerged renewed,
and now I walk forward,
no longer tethered to who I once was.

Violet,
I must see you tomorrow in court,
yet tonight, I yearn for another's arms,
for a woman's embrace
to hold me close and whisper
that everything will be alright.

In this quiet longing,
I seek solace from the storm,
a gentle voice to calm the chaos,
to offer comfort before the dawn.

For though I'll face you tomorrow,
tonight I need a refuge,
a moment of peace
in someone else's presence,
before confronting what lies ahead.

Violet,
one might say we are strangers now
after all this time,
but we both know we aren't.

If we were to talk,
we would have so much to share,
laugh like old friends again,
until the conversation fades,
and we remember the pain,
the lies, the depression,
returning to our hatred for one another.

I am still drifting in numbers
that will never be counted,
lost in the spaces between
who we were and who we've become,
haunted by memories
that linger like a mist,
infinite and unyielding.

V,
12:11 am
I wish you'd walk through my
front door,
come to my bedroom,
crawl into bed with me,
and hold me until I fall asleep.

Your presence, a comforting balm,
would quiet the restless thoughts,
soothing the chaos of the night
until peace drifts in
with the gentle rhythm of your breath.

Getting dressed for court,
where I will have to face
the presence of my abuser,
feels like preparing
for a funeral.

Each garment weighs heavy,
like mourning clothes
for a part of me lost,
for the innocence stolen,
for the peace disrupted.

The mirror reflects
the armor I must wear,
a facade of strength
over the trembling fear,
ready to confront the demons
of what once was.

In this solemn ritual,
I brace for the moment,
hoping for justice,
seeking closure,
as I step into the courtroom,
an uninvited mourner
at the wake of my past.

I left May with a deep resentment
for the entire month,
stepping into June
filled with anxious thoughts,
my reality uncertain,
my mind a storm of manic
and depressive waves.

But Natasha, with her quiet strength,
helped calm the tempest,
soothing my restless spirit,
helping me find balance
amid the chaos.

I will forever be grateful
for her short-lived presence,
a beacon of peace
in my turbulent life,
leaving an indelible mark
even as she drifted away.

As May rolls into June,
I turn the page in my journal,
ready to capture new verses
for a new woman I've met.

Her presence inspires my pen,
lines flowing with the promise
of fresh beginnings,
words blossoming like flowers
in the warmth of early summer.

Each poem is a testament
to the unfamiliar excitement,
as I explore the depths
of this newfound connection,
eager to see where
these lines will lead.

I've gone seven weeks
without filling the void
inside me
by letting a woman's heart
trace its way in.

Each day stretches,
a silent ache that lingers,
as I navigate the emptiness
with patience and resolve,
waiting for the touch
that once soothed
but now feels distant.

In this quiet space,
I learn to embrace
the absence,
to find solace
in the stillness,
and to heal
without the familiarity
of a tender, fleeting connection.

Dawn

I'm weary, and it's well past my bedtime.
We've only been talking for a month,
and though you're still a stranger,
you've given my soul everything it has longed for
without a word from me.

I'm cautious, guarding my heart,
but you've offered what I needed,
unspoken, unasked.

I hope you don't falter—
I hope nothing emerges to stir that uneasy feeling,
the one that tells me something's amiss,
that I should retreat.

May we both find success
and comfort in this fragile connection.

Some days, I think you might be the one
to scale my towering wall.
You'd perch at the summit,
spitting down on those who failed,
mocking their attempts with a rodent's simile,
then leap back down, feet first,
to the other side,
joyful simply to be there.

You don't give me butterflies.
You said the same, and we agreed
they're a bad sign.

I still fear that rushing might unravel us,
so I insist we take our time,
letting our friendship
be a slow, steady flame.

You understand that the cards you hold
are not of your own dealing,
but remnants left by others,
an imperfect hand.

These cards, marked by their past,
are not a winning hand
but a shuffled deck of broken promises
and unspoken regrets.

Yet here you are,
playing with what you've been given,
navigating through the remnants
of what others have left behind.

In the midst of this imperfect game,
your patience and understanding
shine through the cracks,
offering a glimpse of hope
in a hand that wasn't yours to choose.

When I read your texts,
your voice lingers in my mind,
each word spoken with the tone
and warmth you convey.

The rhythm of your speech
translates seamlessly to text,
and as I read, it feels as if you're here,
speaking those words directly to me.

In the quiet of my thoughts,
your voice becomes a soothing presence,
bridging the distance
with the resonance of your true self.

I hesitate to speak in poetry to you,
fearful of the embarrassment it may bring,
afraid you might not understand.

It's as if I'd be peeling back my flesh,
revealing the hidden skeleton
that no one else ever sees.

You wouldn't grasp the depth,
the rawness of what's exposed.
You wouldn't understand.

I'm not romanticizing you,
nor am I chasing you through distant dreams.
I'm not waiting by the window,
hoping for a message that might never come.

I'm reading you,
not through the gloss of fantasy,
but through the quiet pages of reality,
deciphering each nuance and truth.

I'm studying you,
observing the patterns of your heart,
exploring the depth of your being,
with the patience of one who seeks understanding.

I don't understand why
I don't understand.
The puzzle pieces elude me,
shifting just out of reach.

All I know is that my soul
finds clarity in your presence,
as if a deeper truth
emerges when we're close.

In the space between us,
understanding unfurls quietly,
a silent knowing
that bridges what I cannot grasp.

I stopped searching for you,
exhausted by Karmic Loves
draining my spirit,
I ceased my pursuit.

I paused, ready to wait
for however long it took,
content in the knowledge
that you'd arrive when the time was right.

Then, out of the stillness,
you appeared,
inquiring if we might
reconnect tomorrow.

As if you'd been patiently
waiting for me to cease
my search, and in that silence,
find you again.

You said you don't want to lose me,
and strangely, on the same day,
I shared this very fear with a friend—
expressing my worry over not following
the right rules to avoid pain.

The truth is, I've already strayed
from my own guidelines, breaking
the cycle of toxic patterns I once knew.
I've had my fill and moved beyond,
yet today, my friend advised me
to embrace what's unfolding
between us in these nearly two months.

As we grow closer,
I find myself anxious about losing
my cherished solitude.
What if I can't meet your needs,
and am left feeling bound,
responsible for giving all my time
and energy, overwhelmed by the weight
of your expectations?

I will probably fall in love with you.
At this juncture in my life,
after the storms I've weathered,
I've come to see that only soul mates,
karmic loves, and false twin flames
have gifted me with illusory affection.

With you, it's different.
I will probably fall in love with you.
I'm not halting this journey,
but neither am I cloaking you
in idealized illusions.

I'm letting us be.
I'm learning you
and allowing you to learn me.
I'm as open as I can be
with someone I've known
for less than two months.

Had we met at any other moment in our lives,
it would not have been the right time,
and we would not be who we are now—
weaving a bond born of trust,
connection, and friendship.

Our paths, shaped by the passage of time,
have brought us together precisely when
we were ready to build this foundation,
a relationship rooted in the present,
growing from the soil of shared understanding.

We haven't said "I love you"
because we haven't yet fallen in love,
and the irony lies in the depth
of our kindness and compassion.

We nurture each other with patience,
feel safe in our vulnerability,
offer space, and extend unwavering trust.
Plans are made for cherished moments,
and dreams and goals are supported.

In all this, we show profound love,
without the need to utter those words too soon,
allowing our connection to grow
in the quiet grace of understanding.

Short poems about you
transform into paragraphs,
where I try to convey
the depth of my feelings,
without ever saying
"I love you" in those exact words.

Each line and phrase
weaves around the truth,
expressing what words alone
can't fully capture—
the quiet confession
of my heart's affection.

You're not someone I could
learn to love,

but rather someone I could
gently fall in love with.

Like a quiet dawn,
soft and unhurried,
you invite me to unravel
slowly, tenderly,
as if falling in love
is not a choice,
but a natural unfolding.

I'm bitter
about your ex
because she knows you
better than I do
right now.

Her past with you
is a map I can't read,
a language I'm still learning,
while I'm left
tracing unfamiliar lines
of your history,
feeling like a stranger
in the chapters she wrote.

If you decide you want to walk away,
I'll be ready this time,
to carry my heart in a million little pieces,
without losing fragments in the darkness.

I'll gather each shard with steady hands,
bearing the weight of my own resilience,
ready to rebuild from the fragments,
stronger than before,
even if you are no longer here.

I'm so scared you'll learn me
and know me better than I know myself.

That fear haunts me,
for in your understanding,
you might see the darkness I live in,
the demons I try to hide.

And then, I'll push you away,
afraid of how close you've come,
terrified of revealing the depths
I struggle to confront alone.

I'm annoyed by her,
a sensation I can't shake.
I don't want her here,
not for kisses, hugs, or even glances.
I don't want to be touched or speak,
caught in a whirl of conflicting feelings.

I'm uncertain if this is a transient emotion,
a fleeting disturbance in my mind.
I don't trust my own judgments,
wondering if depression or mania shapes my thoughts.

She has been wonderful,
but I question if I've stepped into a relationship too soon.
Did one of my fractured selves push me here?
Am I caught in the cycle of self-sabotage,
unsure if I need space or if she would understand?

Do I need a touch of loneliness
to find peace within myself?
These questions circle,
leaving me adrift in my own uncertainty.

Lacey

Do you love me so deeply
because you doubt that anyone else
could ever love you?
Is our connection
a refuge from the fear
of never being seen again?

I know you would journey
to the end of the Earth
to reveal the depth of your love
for me.

With each step you'd traverse
mountains and seas,
just to show me how boundless
your heart truly is.

I'm absorbing your love
like sunlight soaking into my skin,
each moment deepening my warmth.
Yet, I find myself on the edge of tears,
struggling to find the words
that can truly capture
how profoundly your love affects me.

I'm overwhelmed by the weight of my feelings,
not knowing how to convey
the depth of my gratitude,
how your affection fills every crevice of my soul.
I long to express this boundless appreciation,
but the words elude me,
leaving me both fulfilled and aching,
yearning to show you just how much
I cherish the love you give.

I waited forever for you—
my entire existence stretched thin,
awaiting the day you'd arrive.
Yet, now that you're here,
your presence is bound,
caged by moments and conditions.

The freedom I dreamed of,
of you being with me
whenever I needed,
remains just out of reach.
I am left with the sadness of my longing,
the reality of our time
not matching the eternity
I once envisioned.

I feel like I'll never find the perfect words
to weave together the tapestry of your beauty.
Each attempt falls short,
never quite capturing the depth of what I see.

I want to tell you that every day without you
feels like a void I can't endure,
that my life seems incomplete
without you by my side, always.

In poetry's delicate dance,
I struggle to convey this truth:
You are the breath I need,
the essence of my every day.

We found each other,
lost amidst the riptide of life,
yet our paths converged once more
on the shore,
where we stood drenched
in the echoes of past traumas.

We dried each other's tears,
wounded but healing,
and limped together toward paradise,
where among the trees,
we ignited a fire
that warmed the spaces
between our souls.

I want to reveal to you
what it means to be enveloped
in a love so profound,
it might light up the darkest corners
of your heart and make you happier
than you've ever been.

I want to show you the depth
of my affection,
to wrap you in a warmth
that feels like coming home,
and make you feel cherished
beyond your wildest dreams.

Violet,
will it always be this way?
Will I forever find myself
pondering if you're thinking of me?

If by chance we crossed paths,
would our eyes meet
and conjure every beautiful moment
we've shared?
Would we freeze in that gaze,
reluctant to let it go,
each memory replaying in silence?

Do you find yourself lost
in these thoughts as well?

I feel like I shouldn't be dating someone
while the one I miss still haunts my heart.
How can I give my all to a new love
when my thoughts linger on the remnants
of someone who once filled my soul?

The weight of memories tugs at my heart,
making it hard to embrace the present
when the past still holds its grip
on the path I'm trying to walk forward.

I'm weary of loving a version of her
that I sculpted from dreams and memories,
a fantasy born of my own design,
rather than the truth of who she truly is.

You said I was holding on, waiting to let go—
like all the others before me.
Maybe you were right,
but my truth was that I had no intention
of ever letting go
until you brought that toxic presence
back into your life.

You chose her over me... again.

I barely even wrote about you,
a fleeting presence in my world,
a chapter not destined to be etched in ink,
but merely proof that I still wrestle
with the lessons I have yet to learn.

You were a fleeting trace in the margins,
a gentle reminder that my heart
has not yet mastered the art of letting go,
and the cycle of my struggles
continues to spin.

In the silence of my unspoken words,
your memory lingers as a lesson unlearned,
a testament to the journey I'm still on,
where every encounter, every heartache,
teaches me to find strength in the struggle.

You claimed four months of my heart,
and I thought I owed you some parting words—
a final word of what we had.

But I don't.
I moved on,
even while we were still entwined,
letting go long before the end.

I want to save writing about you for the first of the new year,
like you're so special, deserving of a year dedicated solely to your presence—
as if my current year doesn't hold the energy you deserve.

But you're here,
for reasons beyond our understanding,
and speaking with you feels like meeting a soul I've never encountered in this lifetime.

I fear I stand alone in these thoughts,
my demons whispering doubts,
telling me not to trust myself, that everyone covets my light.

They see my glow, snuff it out,
and then wonder what happened to me,
leaving me to sit in sorrow,
asking why I don't deserve to keep my light.

I do not think I am someone who can truly love.
I'm too much work, too difficult, too complex—
a tangled web of thoughts and emotions
that even I struggle to unravel.

I can feel myself bracing for the moment
you'll see through the façade,
waiting for you to say,
"you're just too much to deal with."

In the quiet moments,
I fear the truth will surface,
and you'll walk away,
leaving me to face the mirror,
seeing the reflection I've long avoided.

Just please be normal—
be yourself, but also
allow me to be exactly
who I am, in all my facets.

Let us meet in the middle,
where authenticity thrives,
and we can be flawed,
yet perfectly real.

In your presence,
let me feel free to unfold,
without the weight of pretense,
just the freedom to be truly me.

My paranoia suggests you're not truly yourself,
that a mask shields what's beneath.
Yet my hope shines through,
believing you're embracing the person you've always
longed to be.

In the tug-of-war between doubt and faith,
I navigate the uncertainty,
hoping to glimpse the genuine you,
and trusting that, perhaps, this is your authentic self
emerging.

I'm always the filler,
the one they turn to
to mask the pain of lost loves.
I never get a fresh start,
a whole heart ready to build with me.

Instead, I stand there,
offering all of myself,
while their soul lingers in the past,
clinging to someone who's no longer theirs.

There I am,
eyes wide, soul bare,
ready to love with every fiber of my being,
but always overshadowed
by the love they still hold
for someone else.

A year of searching in all the wrong places,
and gazing at all the wrong faces,
I found you in the final days,
in a spot I'd deemed hopeless.

Yet there you were,
waiting to welcome the new year together,
a beacon in the twilight,
unexpected and true.

So many times I thought,
"I finally found her,"
but each time revealed
an imposter, a mimic—
a counterfeit, a knockoff
of you.

I wonder if you feel the same
atmosphere exploding around us
when we laugh, or if it's just me,
caught in the cascade of our joy,
where every chuckle seems to ignite
a burst of warmth that dances in the air.

Do you sense the world shift,
as if the universe pauses,
to savor our shared moments,
or is it only my heart
that races with the thrill
of our synchronized laughter?

As our laughter mingles and swirls,
I question if you see the same
magic in these fleeting seconds—
the electric spark that seems to bridge
the space between us,
or if I alone feel this cosmic connection.

Asking you to be my girlfriend
was a daunting leap,
a tremor in my heart
that wavered with fear and longing.
Yet in that moment of vulnerability,
all I desired was for you to be mine.

The fear of rejection
danced on the edge of my courage,
but my heart, raw and open,
yearned for the certainty
of calling you mine,
despite the trembling risk.

In the trembling darkness of doubt,
my desire shone brighter,
a beacon guiding me to you,
hoping you'd see beyond the fear
and step into the space
where my heart so eagerly waits.

And just like that, one year,
and it was over.
It ended before it truly began,
while you grieved the absence of another,
using me to fill the emptiness your sorrow left behind.

You never loved me,
only the notion of someone
being so kind and true.
We were never more than fleeting figures
in each other's lives,
never truly known,
never truly connected.

Dear Self

The more I heal,
the more I uncover
that I am my own worst enemy—
but in the same breath,
I am also my own hero.

I keep asking the universe,
and it keeps providing,
so I tread lightly with this gift,
mindful not to let desire consume me.

I strive to share the light I've received,
returning positive energy to the cosmos,
for whoever's path may cross mine next,
so they too can find the warmth and grace.

The moment I fell in love with myself,
the universe whispered its approval,
bestowing eternal happiness,
as if to say I had finally earned it.

In that self-love, I found the key,
unlocking a future bright and boundless,
where my heart and soul
could bask in their own radiant light.

I didn't know
I was supposed to love myself—
no one told me that,
no one shared the secret.

It was a lesson learned in silence,
a truth discovered alone,
like a hidden gem
shining in the dark.

Dear Self,

You deserve the love you can give yourself—
no warm body can fill the void
you've longed to mend.
Seeking solace in any woman's gaze
was never going to heal
the wounds of real heartbreak.

Take your time.
You are worthy of love,
a love that starts within,
and the gentle embrace
of a woman who sees you whole.

Carolyn Campbell

ABOUT THE AUTHOR

Carolyn Campbell is a passionate poet whose work delves deep into the intricacies of human emotions and relationships. Growing up in a small town, Carolyn developed a keen sensitivity to the world around her, which she channels into her evocative writing. Her poetry explores themes of love, trauma, and self-discovery, often reflecting personal experiences and universal truths.

With a talent for capturing the raw essence of emotion, Carolyn's work resonates with readers seeking authenticity and connection. Her unique voice offers insight into the complexities of identity and healing, inviting readers to embark on a journey of introspection and understanding. *Drifting In Numbers* is Carolyn's first collection, a testament to her ability to weave words into powerful expressions of the human spirit.

Carolyn Campbell

Made in the USA
Columbia, SC
16 September 2024

41877103R10202